The
FRENCH
TUREEN

A NOVEL

Cathy Powers

The French Tureen

ISBN-13: 978-0-578-43595-4
ISBN-10: 0-578-43595-0

TIDING
PRESS

DESIGNED BY
HEATHER POWERS GRAY

TIDINGPRESS.COM

First Edition

Printed in the U.S.A

PREFACE

The French Tureen **is a work of fiction,** although I have drawn upon actual events and stories of my ancestors. There really is a violet-covered French tureen (pictured on this cover) that was passed down to me through at least six generations of grandmothers. All the main characters are fictitious and have no relation to anyone living or dead.

This is dedicated to my great-grandmother, Margaret Fowler Knowles, who truly survived the Civil War in Tennessee and went on to become the strong woman I have referred to in some chapters. More of her life will be revealed in my next book.

CHAPTER ONE

A s I shifted my position in the uncomfortable waiting room chair, I noticed an elderly couple slowly making their way into the large room. The old lady was slightly bent over, using a walker. A very attentive old man hovered at her side, ready to assist. He was far from strong himself, but it only took one glance to know that this was a devoted couple. My imagination told me that they had been married for a very long time and weathered many storms together. When he looked at her, it was obvious he still saw a beautiful young girl. It took this lady a few minutes to make her way into a chair and slowly settle into it. Her mate patted her arm, and I noticed he had been carrying her purse.

This was not the first time for me to both envy and almost hate couples like this. I had seen similar scenes play out many times. I am very touched by seeing a devoted older man treat his wife in this manner, but also consumed by jealousy. I suppose many people would reserve these feelings for young, strong, and beautiful couples. However, the lives of the young ones are still to be played out; they have not endured the test of time. I had experienced this lurch of feelings so many times that it was like a reflex. Noticing I had been reading and re-reading the same page of my book several times, I closed it.

I let my mind wander back through the years, and wondered when I had first learned to choke back the pain. It was far earlier than a young girl should ever have to do this. Like those movies when one can magically travel back and hover over the young person they used to be, I watched my earlier self on a long, hot summer day. I must have been about seven or eight. My grandparents always arose early to get chores finished before the heat of the day, later napping on the front porch. I spent those steamy Indiana afternoons entertaining myself.

I learned to read at a very early age, and also had an active imagination. Perhaps this served to enrich my life, but it also gave me the ability to torture myself. As I had done so many times, I saw myself petting my faithful little dog and heading down the long gravel driveway to my favorite maple tree. It afforded both shade and comfort to that little girl growing up in the 1950s. After all of this time I can still picture the summer haze over the wheat field as I gazed across it.

I observed my own ethnic-looking face and knew just what she was thinking. Perhaps this would be the day a big, expensive car would appear, and my father would be inside. He would turn into the driveway and hold out his arms for me. I would run to him and somehow, magically, he would take my mother and me away with him. I would never be alone again. Of course, the one event that had set in motion all of what was to come later was much further in the past.

Snapping back to the present, I gave up on reading my book. I let myself go back and envision how that fateful day must have happened. As always, I edited in the parts that I really had no knowledge of. I had figured out long ago that the direction of our lives is greatly influenced by events from way before we were born.

Even my active imagination could not travel to the 15th century when my French, Irish, and English ancestors were still in Europe. As usual, I decided to take a mental journey to the antebellum South when my great-grandmother, Maybelle Dupree Chastain, was still on a small plantation in Dresden, Tennessee. Like so many others, the Civil War changed the way of life the Dupree family had taken for granted for generations.

I imagined that beautiful Maybelle, always known as Belle, was called into the parlor by her mother one day and told they had nothing left in Tennessee, and would be moving to southern Illinois. Some cousins lived there who had offered their hospitality until the Duprees could find a way to make a new life.

At this point, my thoughts were interrupted by realizing the sweet old lady was speaking to me.

"Excuse me, dear, but you have such a look on your face that I had to ask. Are you worried about someone in surgery right now?"

I pulled myself back to the reality of the moment, putting on my Kate mask, as I had done for most of my life. I smiled at the couple, and replied.

"Thanks so much for asking, and yes, I am waiting for someone to have surgery. Are you waiting, too?"

At this point, the woman struggled back to her feet, and moved closer to where I was sitting. She motioned for her husband to follow.

"Yes, we are waiting to hear news about our son. He is having heart surgery."

I gave her a look of sympathy and avoided giving any direct reply. I decided I would be honest in another way.

"My name is Kate Williams, and I was actually thinking back to many decades ago, about how my great-grandmother's life was disrupted by the Civil War, and how her family's move to Illinois changed so many lives. I often muse about how history is changed by one small decision."

"I'm Grace Madison, and this is my husband Jack," she said with a smile. I imagined that this was one of about a million times she had beamed at this man. "We have been married for nearly 58 years now. That was the best decision I ever made."

"Grace, I can tell that those have been very happy years for both of you."

"Oh, yes, we have a wonderful family, with our third great-grandchild on the way."

As always, I felt a twinge of envy, as well as many other emotions. I must have let a shadow fall over my face, because she went on to ask another question.

"Kate, is there something you would like to talk about while we all sit and wait? I am a very good listener."

Jack picked up a magazine and settled into his chair with a little smirk. He had seen his still beautiful wife engage strangers in conversation many times before.

I could see that Grace would have been stunning as a young woman. Her snowy white hair must have been blonde long ago, judging by her fair complexion and cornflower blue eyes. The absence of wrinkles on her face suggested that she had avoided frowning most of her life. I hated myself for envying this, too.

I took a deep breath and said, "Well, are you up for hearing a very long story?"

CHAPTER TWO

I had been a very shy child, but now in my sixties, I was oddly able to launch off into a personal narrative about my family to these strangers. Even only knowing this sweet old couple for a few minutes, I was suddenly totally fine with having this conversation. For way too long I had felt the whole thing bubbling to the surface like a ticking bomb. I had considered telling a few others in the past, but it never felt right.

I had worked for years on creating an image, and I never let anyone see the real Kate any more. I had to be the smart, brave little girl. Sometimes, when I was alone, I screamed at God and various dead family members and friends. So many things had been decided when I was a baby. I did not get to vote. I had slowly invented the person that I wanted the world to see. Anything that did not seem to fit was shoved down so deep that I stopped being honest with the world — and most of all — with myself.

How could I have known this lovely lady so briefly and decide to make her the one to hear it all? Almost no one, even close friends, let alone my children, ever saw past the carefully arranged smile I had learned to wear for all to see. I had frequently wondered if they just chose not to acknowledge what I endured, or if they really saw me as such a strong person that they had no guilt in letting me march on alone.

When I had awakened several hours ago, I went through the same motions of almost every morning of my life. I knew that more was required of me today, so I lingered over that first cup of coffee. I let the dogs out into the fenced yard, but they soon wanted back in. Southwestern Indiana was having an unusually cool fall season. I flipped the thermostat up a few degrees and stepped into the shower. The hot water was soothing, and I needed that.

I used to choose my daily outfits with care, but I had fallen into just throwing on something comfortable. It was autumn, so I selected a loosely fitted brown sweater and jeans. My black sneakers would afford me comfort in walking. I had owned the all-weather coat for a long time, and dark brown went with everything.

My once dark hair was streaked with strands of gray as I was long overdue for an appointment at the beauty shop. My brown eyes reflected the inner stress I felt. I still tried to watch what I ate, but I had long given up losing the twenty pounds that I used to worry so much about. Although I was petite in height like my maternal grandmother, I was also built like the Eastern European paternal side that I knew little about.

I fed the sweet dogs and gave them some loving before grabbing my purse, a book, and walking out the door. I scarcely remembered driving to the hospital that morning.

CHAPTER THREE

I hesitated, trying to decide how I could ever really explain all that swirled around in my head so many days of my life. I really could not remember a time when I had not felt the need to continue searching for that intangible thing most people seem to take for granted. So often, I made a mental retreat back to great-grandma Maybelle's life, and tried to picture all that she dealt with. This was really where it all began.

Her life had been changed radically, like thousands of others, by the Civil War. When it ended she was just a child. There had been no choice for her family. They had to leave Tennessee and resettle in a very small town in southern Illinois. By the time she matured into a young woman, Belle was happily working for her cousin, Bruce, in his grocery store. It wasn't much, just a little place where locals could buy the basics. After the War, small farmers from both the North and South experienced hard economic times. Belle came from generations of proper ladies who were as tough as they were beautiful. Her French heritage had given her the coal black hair, tiny frame, and huge dark eyes that would be passed down for generations to come.

There was a lot of time for her to sit on the high stool and just daydream. Many of her spare minutes were spent doing the fine needlework she had learned as a child. She also enjoyed tending the family's small garden. Upon leaving her childhood home, Belle had seen her mother carefully harvest important seeds to replant in Illinois, as well as small jars of dried mushrooms and herbs.

It was on such an afternoon that a young stranger wandered into town. Seeing the store, he tied his horse to the hitching post and entered, seeking a cool drink. A petite, raven-haired beauty in a faded blue dress met his eyes as he walked inside. His breath caught. The man had never seen bigger eyes or a smaller waist. It was a vision he would never forget.

Arthur Chastain was a bit of a rake. He wasn't big on normal jobs involving labor. Fortunately for him, he had musical talent and the gift of gab. The guitar strapped across his saddle had helped him earn many a meal. Small taverns had begun to spring up across the farmlands in the Midwest, and he visited many of them. There was much for men to forget after the brutal war years, and a few stiff drinks got them through the hard days. If Arthur wasn't playing or singing for the regulars, he was good at finding a card game to engage in. He also found that a drink or two made his days complete.

When I was a child, I was told most of these facts, but I could only imagine the conversation that ensued that summer afternoon. He turned on his charm and Belle undoubtedly smiled and blushed. Arthur finished his drink, climbed on his horse, and rode away. The next town had a lively tavern and he wanted to be there before sunset. Belle found herself trembling and stuck her slender finger with the needle, leaving a small drop of blood on the linen she was embroidering.

Arthur always said that his horse had decided which road he should take, but he found himself back at the little store on his return trip to Indiana. Belle felt her heart quicken when she saw him enter. More flirting went on before Arthur reluctantly got back on his horse.

Since their migration to the north, Belle's parents had gotten jobs to help their family survive. She always admired her father, Benjamin, who had been a respected landowner before the war. He now was forced to work as hard as the small group of slaves they had once owned. His brave wife, Lucy, had survived those dark days in her own way while her husband was away. She baked pies and cakes to sell to some of the families in their new town. Connersville was growing again, and farming was the way money came along for most families. Some far-sighted men had bought up lots of land, and they were becoming rich. Belle's brother had fallen at Gettysburg and probably was buried in a mass grave.

In the coming weeks, Belle found herself watching down the dusty street, hoping to see the dashing stranger return. As a child in Tennessee, she had seen a lot of Southern gentlemen with their polite manners. Arthur was nothing like anyone she had ever met.

Summer turned toward autumn, and this was normally the time when Arthur kept his ventures much closer to home. Fighting the deep snows of winter did not work for him. Prosper, his small southern Indiana hometown, had a tavern where he played his violin and guitar, and he lived in a humble room upstairs. His talent was appreciated and the old hat on the floor always had a little money thrown into it. In return for room and board — and a stable for his horse — he acted as bartender for the owner.

However, this year he found himself taking the small ferry to cross the Wabash River much later than he had done in past years. There were many more stops at the little store.

Knowing he had no other place to go, Belle impulsively asked Arthur to share their meager Thanksgiving dinner. The family gathered around the weathered oak table that had traveled with them from Tennessee, and all gave thanks for the meal.

On impulse, Arthur stood up so quickly that his chair fell over, turned to Benjamin, and blurted out, "I love your daughter, sir, and I want to take her back to Indiana with me!"

I am not sure anyone ever ate another bite of that meal. Belle sat quietly, hearing everyone talk all at once, and the discussion seemed to go on forever. In later years she could not remember exactly what was said, but on the day after Christmas she stood in the small parlor wearing a crumpled ivory dress that was once her mother's, and was wed. After tears and hugs, they strapped her carpetbag onto the horse and the couple set off east for Indiana.

After living through a long and cold winter in the tiny, drafty room above Prosper's only tavern, Belle insisted they find another place to stay. She also insisted that Arthur look for a steady job. A house came up for rent out on North Street, and they moved. Belle began to take in laundry and sewing for others. Arthur worked at the train station, delivering packages that arrived on the morning train. They borrowed a wagon and returned to Illinois to bring back some of the family furniture that had come from Tennessee. Belle insisted on having the marble top dresser that had always been in her bedroom. She also wanted the porcelain soup tureen from France. Covered in violets, it was the very thing in which her mother had once served mushroom soup to the Yankees.

When warm weather returned Arthur felt the need to travel again, so he was gone much of the time. However, he did come back with much needed money, so Belle tried to understand. When he slipped into the big feather bed and pulled her into his strong embrace, she tended to forgive him for his long absences. It wasn't long before she became pregnant, making the extra income even more necessary.   The first little boy was followed by another, and twin daughters came along in the Spring of 1886. The baby born first, Frances, would become my grandmother. She was always the dominant twin, never letting her sister Frieda forget who was oldest.

Grace had listened to me relate this tale from the past without uttering a word. Her husband was sound asleep, taking soft breaths. She automatically reached out and patted his hand.

After a minute or two she turned back to me and said, "Well, go on — there must be more!"

CHAPTER FOUR

Whenever I allow myself to go back in time and think about my great, great grandmother, I always picture a woman of immense strength. On the fateful day Lucy observed the three Yankee soldiers riding down the dirt road to her Tennessee home, it was obvious she must do whatever was necessary. She had spent a lifetime of figuring out how to survive. Her husband was still off with the other Confederate volunteers from Weakley County, but she bravely stood on the shady front porch to greet the soldiers in dark blue uniforms. Lucy's heart still ached recalling the day she had been notified that her only son, Will, had fallen at Gettysburg. However, she had long heard the stories of how her mother and grandmother had endured many hard times. Being able to survive everything was her legacy.

Belle was only nine years old when the Union soldiers rode down the lane, but that day must have been seared permanently into her head. Even as a child, she had been taught to fear the Yankees, so she was surprised when her mother offered them a meal. Soon, Lucy was busy stirring up soup, using her little jar of dried mushrooms along with some of the remaining vegetables from the garden. When Belle awoke the next morning, the soldiers were gone. It was much later in her life before she surmised what must have happened.

I turned back to Grace and tried to describe Belle's life, desperately searching for the words to fully convey the real story. I never got to meet Belle, because she already lay in her grave in the cemetery just north of town by the time I was born. I am just glad I have the faded photos of her to help picture those long past years. I related the early courtship of Belle and Arthur as best I knew it..

"Belle was the strongest woman I have ever heard about, and when I talk about her, I still wonder how she kept her strength throughout all of her ninety-two years. Much of this story, Grace, was told to me in many different ways, from my grandmother and several different people. However, I actually have a handwritten account I found years later in her ragged family bible."

Grace replied, "Yes, dear, that was the way much of a family's history was passed down. They didn't have the internet!"

"I was lucky to get this bible back into the family, actually. A good friend owned an antique store and was always buying large lots of things at estate sales. One day she came to see me, carrying a huge bible with yellowed pages and a badly damaged cover. It was bulging with newspaper clippings, old photos, and other papers. My friend had read enough of the contents to figure out it belonged in our family. If someone else had bought it, I would never have seen it."

"Whenever I had some time I looked through the items it contained. A narrative of births and deaths gave me information that I did not know. When I was a child, I listened to my grandmother, Frances, and her twin sister, Frieda, discuss the past on long afternoons, sitting on the cool front porch. I don't remember their conversations as much as I wish I could. I do know that it always seemed to be an argument. Most twin sisters are close from birth, but my tiny grandmother was the dominant sister. They were beautiful in their youth, but years of hard work had taken its toll. Frances had long gray hair which she put up on her head by rolling it with a pencil and securing it with those old-fashioned hair pins."

"My aunt Frieda had decided to use horrible black hair color that was available at old dime stores, and for as long as I knew her, it made her damaged hair have a slightly purple tint. It rubbed off on her collars and she was as thin as anyone could possibly be. Most days she still wore black dresses that seemed to be decades old. This habit started when the love of her life, Dewey, passed away. She never had children and spent much of her time alone."

Grace nodded her head and said," Yes, honey, World War II left a lot of widows. I remember how many of them lived on our street. After their children grew up, they spent much of the last years of their lives quite lonely. I often went to visit them and they were glad of the company. I didn't mind the cookies they gave me, either," she said with a little laugh.

I went on with my story at this point. "Listening to these old ladies argue away many a summer afternoon gave me a lot of information about their history. They mentioned names and events that became familiar to me, but it was difficult to put it all together. After reading through that old bible, I finally figured out how some of it fit into the puzzle."

"The Second World War did influence our family, but not because of the deaths. I guess that almost everyone's life was changed in some way. Wait — I have gotten ahead of my story, and before we talk about the twins as old ladies, I have to tell you what happened decades earlier."

"Going back to their mother, Belle, I could never understand how she managed to raise her children with the meager finances she had at her disposal. I have old photographs that show how her girls went out to parties wearing the loveliest white dresses with lots of handwork. Their clothing looks like the costumes that would have been created by a designer for a period movie. Grandma Frances always told me that people judged you by your appearance, and one's hair and shoes should be immaculate."

"Being born in the South, I am sure these values were instilled into Belle's head early in her life. Even when they no longer had their group of slaves after the War, they kept up appearances and shouldered the work that was once done for them. I still have a lot of the needlework she made. The detail is amazing."

"So anyway, it did not take Belle long to figure it out when Arthur was drinking more and more. She had suspicions of his seeing other women during his travels. Soon she found herself with five children to care for after a little sister named Nell came along to join the family. As soon as the boys were old enough, they found odd jobs that helped the family finances."

"It must have been around this time that the attractive Southern woman became gaunt, her youth long in the past. From taking in sewing and laundry to selling products from the garden, Belle did all that she could. Her teenaged daughters had inherited musical ability from their free-spirited father, and they were much in demand to sing and play the violin, the guitar, and the piano at parties. Belle took pride in seeing their beauty and made sure they had all that she could give them."

"As the boys turned into young men, they inherited their father's love of drinking. The eldest, Nathan, found a small house, not much more than a shack, near his mother. He survived by holding part time jobs, becoming well known for the prize-winning sweet potatoes he planted. His brother James left for the big city. He had Arthur's gift of gab and worked in Chicago selling shoes. As for Nell, I will get to her story later. It plays heavily into much that was to come."

At that point, a doctor, still in his scrubs, came into the waiting room. Grace's face changed to one of concern and took her husband's hand.

"Don't worry, folks, Charlie came through the surgery fine.

However, he will have several days here before we can release him. He will also have to change his ways. No more smoking and careless eating. Losing a few pounds will prolong his life. You can see him now."

I could see that the old couple was greatly relieved, and they started towards the door. As she started into the hall, Grace turned to me.

"I hope you get good news too, Kate. We will probably see you later on, or maybe tomorrow. Our son Charlie is only in his fifties, and sons are not supposed to go before their parents. He went through a bad divorce last year. I hope he can get his life back on track now."

I stood up and gave her a quick hug. Then, once again, I was alone in the room. I suddenly realized I had not even told them I was waiting for my husband, David, to have surgery. My story was so different.

CHAPTER FIVE

Through the years, as I grew up and began to more fully understand all of the events and people who had influenced my life from the beginning and evidently, would until the end, I ardently wished I could travel back in time and fix things. Movies and television shows allow a person to actually do so, but of course, real life does not. It took me years to accept the fact that altering even one small thing would change many lives, and not necessarily for the better.

It wasn't long before a nurse appeared in the doorway. "Mrs. Williams, David is back in his room if you'd like to see him."

Of course, I followed her down the hall and walked into still one more hospital room. I looked down at the sleeping man lying in the bed, now hooked up to various tubes and machines to monitor his vital signs. He looked so small, not at all the strong, vigorous man I used to know. I thought I had already cried all that I could, but tears began to roll down my cheeks. I sat quietly and listened to the noises of the hospital for a while. A large food cart rolled noisily down the hall, and visitors for other patients walked by.

An orderly stuck his head in and asked if I wanted the television to be turned on, but I shook my head. The man in the bed would have wanted it on in years past, but he would not know about that now. I looked at his hands, and more tears came when I pictured all the things those hands had done. The nurse came in and started trying to wake David up to check his vital signs. I knew he would look at me with confusion, as always. She assured me he was doing fine.

The rush of memories soon became too much, and I decided it was time to go. I didn't even realize evening had arrived until I stepped outside. Time seems to stand still in hospitals.

Upon entering the parking lot I had to remind myself which vehicle I was looking for. I no longer needed the large SUV, and had traded it off for a small car. This in itself was one of the concessions that I had been forced to make over the past few months. For decades I had driven many larger trucks and vans, and I didn't really feel right in this economy sedan. My children had suggested I shouldn't be driving anymore at all, but I was far from ready to have that taken away.

Even the small house I now called home still felt like the wrong place, but I had accepted this change. It was nice to drive into the garage and unlock the door. I always smiled when I heard the dogs jump up to greet me. The two aging Shih Tzus were the last in a long series of dog companions we had owned and loved through the years. Mollie was now having a hard time getting around, but her younger companion Daisy still had lots of pep. I gave them fresh water and poured food into their two dishes. They were happy to run out into the small fenced backyard for a few minutes.

I quickly fixed a small salad and sat down to eat it. I hadn't eaten since an early lunch at the hospital cafeteria, which seemed to be a long time ago. I desperately wanted a cup of coffee, but I needed to sleep, and settled for herbal tea. I changed into a pair of oversized pajamas then sank down into my recliner. As expected, the dogs were ready to come in and jump on my lap. Another day in my life was over.

It was around 3 a.m. when I awoke with a start. I had been

having a very vivid dream, one that seemed so real. I had been asleep in the dream, with the voices of my children prodding me to get up. They sounded just like they did all those years ago. I thought I could feel David lying beside me. I even turned to look, but, of course, that was not the case. I frequently had dreams that were rooted in the past. I suppose our subconscious takes us back to happier times. It is always so sad when we wake up and realize that it was only a dream.

I guess hindsight is always like this, but there were so many things I fretted about during those long-past years. There was no way I could have envisioned how my life would be now. What is it they say? We make plans and God laughs? I am not sure that is the exact quote, but nothing had turned out the way I thought it would. David and I had often spoken of how nice our old age would be. Work years would be at an end, we would have a nest egg, and we planned to see the country. We talked about getting a travel trailer, like so many senior citizens do. We discussed where to go and tried to concoct a plan. This was one subject we could agree about, and it seemed like a good reward.

David could no longer remember planning for those days, or much of anything else. I almost thought he was the lucky one. I had noticed his memory slipping more than a decade before, but for a long time, I had tried not to worry about it. When he awoke today at the hospital he would not recall nor understand the procedure he had undergone. I would walk into the room and he would wonder who I was. I tried to remind him every day, as I had for some months now, but sometimes it made him upset, so I found it best to say as little as possible. However, our history of bickering had also gone away.

It was likely a blessing he hadn't been there to witness the auction. I had to let the big house go, along with many of our possessions. Our life there only existed in photographs now. I had steeled myself to make the change for a long time before it actually happened. For a time, I had paid others to come and tend the large yard David had taken such pride in. My son, Eric, had tried to help as much as he could, but it was obviously a burden he did not deserve. Holly called from Florida several times a week, but she too had her own busy life.

I remembered that last day I spent in the old, familiar house. I strolled around the yard, saying goodbye to the mature trees and shrubs we had planted all those years ago. I hoped the new owners would not cut many of them down with no regard for leaving all the birds and squirrels without a home. I had faithfully put out food for them every year and wished someone else would continue to do so. I now avoided driving past my former home. It was just too heartbreaking to do so. The nice young couple who bought it would probably have made changes, and I could not deal with that. They would raise their own children there, creating their own memories. I could not allow myself to picture all the years of my life spent living there. The ghostly voices from the past surely must echo down the hall. Common sense always reminded me that many people had gone through this same change in their lives. But the thought never made me feel all that much better.

That had been one of the saddest days of my life, although there had been many others. I wasn't sure I would survive so many other abrupt changes in the past, but I always did. When I needed to summon up some strength, I went back to remembering how the other strong women in my family had gone on.

I was kind of hoping that I would see Grace again later today. It had been very cleansing to hear myself tell the old story, and there was so much more.

I knew that sleep would not come again, so I got up, made coffee, and opened the door to see if the paper had arrived. Those two habits had started my day for as long as I could remember.

Soon I saw the dark sky begin to lighten. Another day of my life was about to begin.

CHAPTER SIX

O n the way back to the hospital that morning I picked up a couple of doughnuts. I didn't know if David would be able to eat them, or if he would even be awake. Bringing him familiar treats was the only way I could actually contribute to his current life. I thought back to all the bags of doughnuts he had brought home, and this was still another trigger for sad memories.

I entered the room as quietly as possible, noticing that David was looking directly at me. I told him about the doughnuts and sat down by the bed. After a few minutes he asked if I was his nurse. I found it easiest to just nod my head. The actual nurse came in smiling a few moments later.

"Mrs. Williams, he is doing fine. His procedure was not a big deal, and he will only have to be here a few days."

David continued to look at us with confused eyes. I remained a few more minutes but soon returned to the waiting room. I wanted to stay longer, but it was just easier to be in another room.

I took out my book again, thinking I might get back to reading it. I had barely opened it when I saw Grace and Jack slowly walking down the hall. She spotted me sitting there. I suppose that this was the real reason I decided to sit in that same chair, instead of David's room. I desperately wanted to resume our conversation.

"Oh, honey, we are glad to see you again," Grace said. "Our son is resting right now, so we are going to wait around for a while. How is it going with you?"

I decided to explain the situation with David. I saw concern spread over her face after I told her the basic facts. I went on to tell them that in a few days, he would be transferred back to the long-term care facility, Pine Haven.

"Oh, what a terrible way to have to live," she said. "My neighbor lingered on that way for years."

I explained that I didn't visit him every day anymore, no matter how guilty I felt.

"Kate, we were just going to get a little bite to eat; why don't you come with us?"

I had eaten a small breakfast, but going with them seemed much better than sitting alone once again.

We slowly progressed toward the cafeteria and were soon enjoying chicken salad on croissants with steaming cups of coffee. Grace was only two bites in before she asked, "Why don't you tell us the rest of the story today?"

I had to stop and think about where I had left off.

I began by saying, "Grace, I suppose that hearing these stories from so long ago seems strange, but my life always feels like the chapters of a book. Skipping ahead does not explain the last part. I am always thinking about how one small change way back then would have altered so much. But I am sure that is true of almost everyone's life."

Grace nodded knowingly in agreement, and assured me that she wanted to hear it all.

"Well, let me tell you about my grandfather, Henry. He was the eldest son of a wealthy farmer, but he ended up having to make his own way. His mother passed away young, and his father re-married. A little half-brother came along and became the family favorite. After his father's death, Grandpa received enough money to buy his own small farm. However, he was still a young man, attending area parties and picnics with the other single folks. That was the way to find wives back then. They often made the rounds of area church socials and other gatherings."

"My grandmother and her twin sister were in attendance at many of these events, and Frances caught the eye of Henry Harrington right away. Both sisters were beautiful, but Frieda was the quiet sister, so he was centered on Frances. Painfully shy, he finally asked her to go riding that next Sunday in his buggy, pulled by one of his favorite horses."

"She had a bit of a Southern accent — picked up from her mother — which sounded very different to Henry's ears. Almost immediately he began to call her "Dutchie," meaning she was hard to understand. This nickname would stick for all her life. Frances was always jealous of her sister, so she made sure to tell Frieda to stay away from her new beau."

"After a few months of courting, Henry proposed, and they were married on Thanksgiving Day. They moved into a modest farmhouse, and Frances became a farm wife. Belle had made sure her daughters were good cooks with all the skills necessary to be good wives. In about two years their first child, Victoria, was born. She was to become my mother."

"It wasn't long before Frieda also was dating a young man from a neighboring town. He had always been a sickly mama's boy and his mother was not happy to have Frieda in her son's life. Dewey even shared the Chastain name, because he and Frieda were distant cousins. His sister Nola was a large, unattractive girl who had hoped her brother would remain at home, unmarried. Frieda knew from the beginning that she would never win the approval of this woman, but she came to love Dewey, and they were married in a quiet ceremony."

"Dewey and Frieda bought property at the other end of Gibson County and built a house. Dewey had weak lungs, so they hired others to farm their land. This farm was in an area

dotted with working oil wells, so Dewey allowed many oil leas-
es, hoping to cash in. Due to his chronic lung condition they
began to spend part of their winters in Florida. It wasn't long before Frieda realized that she would probably never be a mother."

"Belle was happy her twins were married and settled down,
with the beautiful Nell still at home. Arthur continued to do
small jobs around town, bringing in a meager wage. Due to her
skillful budgeting, Belle was able to get by. After my mother
was born, Belle was frequently asked to go out to the farm and
help out. In the busy summer months, she didn't have much
time to spend with her little girl. It wasn't long before Frances
realized she was going to have another baby. Those were the
days when mothers always hoped for a boy. Not only would
the husband have someone to help with the work, a boy would
carry on the family name."

We had finished the chicken salad sandwiches, so I asked if
Grace and Jack would like to find a more comfortable place to
sit. We decided on the solarium with wide windows. I noticed
a light snow had begun.

"My, my, snow before Thanksgiving usually means a bad winter," Jack observed. Grace usually did all the talking so I was surprised to hear him speak. He was draping a light sweater around
Grace's frail shoulders, and I imagined he did this automatically.

"I hope I am not boring you with this long tale," I said. "I
told you it was not quickly told."

"Oh, no, dear," Grace replied, "I have to hear the rest now."
Jack picked up the newspaper and settled into the soft blue
chair by the window.

"My mother, little Victoria, was barely two when baby
Aaron was born. Even though this new baby occupied most
of whatever spare time her mother had, Victoria was happy to
have a little brother. She ran to his basket whenever he cried
and patted him. He had been born in the hot July of 1913, and
this was the busiest time on the farm. When he was about a

month old, several other farmers converged on the Harrington farm to help bring in the last of the wheat crop. There would be lots of hungry men to feed, plus other chores, so Frances sent word to her mother, asking for her to come and help."

"I have heard the story of this day told so many times I feel I can picture it just as it must have happened. Arthur hitched up the horse to his cart and took his wife the three miles to his daughter's home. It was an extremely humid day, and Belle arrived to find a red-faced, crying baby. She also knew that she would have to help prepare the noontime meal. Victoria adored her grandmother and followed her, looking for attention."

"Belle quickly made up some fruit pies to bake and put them into the iron oven. Frances had mentioned that a few pans of biscuits should be ready for the meal, so Belle dusted the table with more flour. She had been soothing the baby as she worked, but it came to her that Aaron must be thirsty on this warm morning."

"She poured a cup of water from the granite bucket for herself, but hesitated and held the cup first to the baby's lips. Having raised her own babies, Belle knew the water should be boiled and cooled for young children, but thought a few swallows couldn't hurt that much. As the busy day progressed, she repeated this action several times. She sat Victoria down with a cool glass of buttermilk and a big piece of cornbread."

"As the day was ending, the work done, Belle cleaned up the kitchen. Frances finally had time for the children. She gave Victoria a hug before turning her attention to the baby. Belle heard her daughter scream, and turned to see her holding a lethargic baby covered with the evidence of severe dysentery. A doctor was sent for, but by the time he arrived at the farm, it was too late."

"Although he had only been granted a month of life on this earth, baby Aaron's death would affect many lives even generations later. Much could be traced back to this day. Long before I even knew all of this, I often visited his small grave at the cemetery and stroked the concrete lamb on top of his tombstone."

CHAPTER SEVEN

"When a death occurred in those times, funerals were held in the family home. It had to be done in haste, especially in the summer. A kindly neighbor quickly built a small wooden casket for the poor baby, and he was laid in the parlor. By noon the following day, groups of friends and church members arrived carrying baskets of food. Frances had retired to her bed with some sleeping powder given to her by the doctor. Poor Henry was beside himself with grief, both for his tiny son, and for seeing his beloved wife fall apart."

I noticed that tears had formed in Grace's blue eyes and she was leaning forward to hear every word.

"It hadn't taken Belle long to figure out her part in the boy's death, but she kept it to herself. It would be years later before she disclosed what she had done. She was consumed by guilt after Aaron died that evening, but knew what she had to do. She packed up a few things for Victoria and took her back to town for the night. She was so filled with emotion that she did not try to explain anything to the little girl."

"As soon as morning arrived Belle arose after a nearly sleepless night and fixed some breakfast for Victoria. She combed and braided the girl's hair and washed her face. Belle still owned a black mourning dress she had worn a few years ago when her mother had passed away. It was heavy and stiff for a summer day, but there was no question that she should wear it."

"Arthur was snoring in a chair on the porch. It was evident he had greeted the day with swigs of alcohol to dull his own grief. Belle prodded him awake and they proceeded back to the farm. By the time they arrived there were many wagons and buggies in the yard. The house was stuffed with sweating people. As soon as the minister arrived, there would be a short service."

"My grandfather Henry helped his weeping wife to a small parlor chair. Belle had lifted Victoria off the wagon, and she immediately ran into the house. With so much else to think about, Belle assumed that she would just go to her mother. However, Henry shooed Victoria away, telling her that mommy couldn't hold her right now. Nobody was really watching her, so she walked right up to the strange wooden box that had appeared."

"My poor confused mother was shocked to see her baby brother inside that box. It did not seem right to her. Nobody seemed to be taking care of him. She reached over and lifted him out, asking, "Why is good baby in box?""

"Silence fell over the room. No one knew what to do. At last, Henry walked to his little girl, took the baby's body out of her arms, and put him back in his tiny casket. Frances passed out on the floor. Running back to his wife, he called for Belle to take Victoria back to her home in town."

"In the next hour, after the minister had said a few hasty words, Frances received more meds and went back to her bed while a long procession of horse drawn vehicles slowly went to the cemetery. Perhaps it was a blessing she never had to watch her baby be lowered into a small grave. This image was seared into Henry's mind for the rest of his life."

"Victoria was confused and sobbing against her grandmother's thin body. Nothing was said on the trip to town. Heat hung heavily over the fields and it was an uncomfortable journey in all ways. Henry had his hands full for days dealing with his own emotions, comforting and caring for his wife, and automatically doing the necessary chores on the farm. Food from the neighbors arrived every day, but he didn't have much of an appetite. Sugary pies and cakes sat rotting on the kitchen table."

"Even Belle did not attempt to explain the situation to Victoria, despite the fact that she was left in her care for more than two weeks. When the little girl cried for her mother, Belle just comforted her and rocked her to sleep. She was fed, bathed, and kept safe, but it was a time of trauma that would be buried in her subconscious. Nell had been staying across town with a friend since the death, so they were alone. Arthur drank from his old flask more than usual, and Belle was weighed down by the entire thing. Although she was only in her sixties, she felt very old. Emotions about everything changed whatever was left of this once vivacious girl into a thin-lipped imitation of her former self. She became even thinner and her calico dresses hung on her tiny frame."

"Aunt Frieda and Uncle Dewey had come for the burial, but instead of turning to her sister for support, Frances made her feel unwelcome. They had their own farm to run, so they returned home. James was too far away to attend. When it was finally determined that Victoria should return to her country home, she found a mother who would never seem quite the same. Frances made sure the girl was cared for, but it was usually Henry who gave her love. Frances sank into a deep depression. It gradually got somewhat better, but Henry did not force her to return to the former daily life and chores for a long time. She soon decided that having another child was the most important thing she could do. It was well over a year before she became pregnant again, but she was determined that she would never fail this coming baby. She prayed for another boy."

"During all those months, Victoria realized her little brother was dead and never coming back. She was raised on a farm and had seen one of the kittens die, so she knew what it meant. She also began trying to please her mother in any way she could. Her child's reasoning was that if she were very, very good, Frances would be happy and loving again. The once happy, carefree toddler became a quiet 4-year-old playing alone in her room. Henry realized this but had no idea how to help. In the spring, he gave her a pet lamb which was a great comfort."

"When the new baby boy arrived, his care was Frances' main concern. She did not let him out of her sight. Named Jesse after her great-grandfather, this child was indulged and spoiled. If Victoria even did the smallest thing, she was spoken sharply to. She found herself spending more and more time in town, in Grandma Belle's care. Belle doted on the little girl. She took some of her carefully hoarded money out of an old sock in the marble topped dresser, and they walked uptown to the grocery."

"Having been raised on home-cooked farm food like fried chicken and canned vegetables, it was a treat for Victoria to have a thick slice of bologna and some crackers out of the big barrel. These outings were to remain happy memories for the rest of her life. She was drawn to her beautiful Aunt Nell and they became close."

CHAPTER EIGHT

"During all her childhood years, it became commonplace for Victoria to accept more chores and receive less attention. By the time she was a teenager, she had a crippling inferiority complex. In addition to her role as the 'girl' at home, her brother Jesse had a sharper mind, and she heard constant praise about him both at home and at school."

"In part due to a cruel math teacher in high school and other influences, Victoria flunked algebra. In later years, she would recall how Mrs. Blasé would berate her in front of the other students. The more she did this, the more Victoria formed a mental block about math. This was just one more thing that made her feel her life would be sad and unfulfilled. She didn't even realize how beautiful she was."

By this time, Grace was biting her lower lip and shaking her head. I took a deep breath and went on.

"Jesse had allergies and asthma, so his doting mother let him sit on the front porch and read novels while his sister had to mow the front yard. This, of course, did not excuse her from performing other household chores. There was always a lot of cooking to do on the farm, so she became an accomplished baker. Her pie crusts were light, flaky, and delicious. I can taste them now."

"It wasn't long before the town gossips began to call her brother the 'white shirt' boy. Even in the early years of the Depression, his mother, Frances, made sure he went out in snow-white shirts. This was a time when so many neighbors were struggling to survive, and it became obvious to lots of people that this was one spoiled boy. He was even allowed to start smoking."

"Even during that dark decade in America, the family had ample food due to raising their own vegetables and having livestock. However, Henry's once wealthy father had invested much of his savings before the stock market crash, and lost the big farm."

"Cash was in short supply, but Henry went out and got jobs on the side in addition to all of the farm work. He was a favorite school bus driver, as well as a grave digger."

"If there was occasionally some spare cash, it enabled Jesse to go out with his friends. However, if Victoria wanted even some change to go to the drugstore with her friends and get a soda, her request was met with frowning disapproval."

At this time, Grace and Jack had to leave, so I was left to my own thoughts. Even though I knew the story so very well, it always stirred my emotions to think about it once again.

I gathered up my things and wandered down the hall to David's room. I slowly entered and found him awake. By now, I was used to the questioning stare that he always gave me.

He immediately started complaining about how much he hated strawberry Jell-O and wanted lime instead. I tried to gently tell him that I would ask at the desk. "What kind of nurse are you?" he snarled.

I again attempted to use patience and calm him down. However, in a moment of strength, this frail old man hurled the unwanted Jell-O at me. It landed squarely on my white blouse and dribbled down the buttons, leaving a pink, sticky trail.

This behavior was not unusual, but it never failed to bring quick tears to my eyes. David had been hospitalized to do minor surgery on his lower left leg, trying to restore some better circulation. He had suffered with this chronic condition for a long time, but it had worsened as he became more and more inactive. It required extra monitoring because he was at risk of developing blood clots.

Forgetting all about the Jell-O, he turned his attention to the very loud television set. "Get my show! Nobody gets my show! Ask my wife; she knows the one! WHERE IS MY WIFE?"

Still wiping the Jell-O off my blouse, I turned and left. You would think that none of this could affect me any longer, I sadly mused. It had been a slow process, and for a long time, I had told myself he was just getting older. I let the events of how David had come to be in the care center rush through my mind that afternoon.

Even after all of this time, I was still wondering if I had done the right thing. As I walked to the parking area, I silently reviewed how it had all progressed.

Never an easy-going person, David's bouts of temper were not surprising. However, there came the day when I found him setting fire to a large pile of crumpled newspaper in the middle of the living room floor.

I met with our primary physician the next day and he referred us to a specialist. I had to lie to David to get him to that appointment. Dr. Wilson was used to dealing with this sad disease and took charge of the big decision. His office secretary took our insurance information and checked the coverage.

Many times I had been thankful for the excellent supplement we had chosen to balance out Medicare. David was immediately cleared to enter Pine Haven, which was only a few miles away. I called the children and told David we were going to check out a vacation place. I expected a hard time getting him to understand what was going on.

The staff at this peaceful facility were experts at handling this hurdle of our life, and it went reasonably well. He liked the yard and they let him taste the food, so he actually wanted to stay. I had already packed him a bag hoping that this would be the day I had both dreaded and prayed for.

As I did the paperwork connected with officially making him a resident there, David strolled over to another old man sitting in the lobby and struck up a conversation. For a brief moment I thought he seemed fairly normal and that I was making a huge mistake. I had seen him talk to people like this for years. However, I soon heard him say he was only here for the night, and that he had to go to work in the morning. He went on to describe the teaching he had done a decade earlier. He bragged about how his students were so very lucky to have him, and even referred to a couple of them who had gotten good jobs right out of college. It had always been important to him to feel his skills made a difference.

I decided this was much like taking a 6-year-old to Kindergarten for the first time — a swift exit was a good way to end this day. It was a very surreal walk to the parking lot. When I got into the SUV, I had never felt so alone. Despite all our differences, he had always been there. I was on my own.

On that summer evening as I turned my vehicle onto the road that would take me back to the house where we had shared so much, I realized my life with my husband had changed forever. Even after a couple of years, this was still not easy. I had never lived alone prior to that day.

I hardly remembered any of this drive home, and it was the happy yapping of the dogs when they heard my key in the door that brought me back to conscious thought.

After feeding the dogs I brewed a cup of decaf and toasted a piece of wheat bread. I made a small bowl of instant oatmeal with a few added blueberries. I ate this quietly, sitting at the table, staring at the wall. I automatically washed out my dishes, put them in the drainer, then moved to the sofa.

When the first rays of sun came in through the French

doors I awoke, realizing I had slept lying on the couch fully clothed. I turned on the shower and stood under the warm water for a long time. Before reaching for the rose-covered towel, I stood there sobbing until there were no more tears. I was not to cry again for a long time. There was too much to do.

CHAPTER NINE

I t was my lifelong habit to make lists, so I reached for a pad of yellow legal paper and started to think of the many tasks I needed to tackle in the next few weeks. Before I had left Pine Haven, the administrator pulled me aside and suggested I not visit for a few days, so that David could settle in. She promised to notify me of any problems. My first call of the day was to just check and see if all was okay.

I asked to speak to Mrs. Trainer and was almost immediately connected. She seemed so young to have this job. Before meeting her the previous evening I had pictured someone like Kathy Bates. The petite blonde who had escorted me into her office did not seem to fit the mold. I saw photos of her children and husband on the desk, so she must be older than she appeared.

I identified myself and she assured me David was doing fine. I had somehow expected him to be very angry and asking for me to show up so that he could scream at me. I was told everything was okay and I wasn't needed for a few days. I later learned Dr. Wilson had ordered some mild meds to make this time easier for David to accept. I never knew if those pills were the reason, but I noticed a significant change in his general demeanor in the next few months. His memory was rapidly declining, and he sat for long periods of time, saying nothing.

My next call was to our attorney. I arranged an appointment and took a deep breath as I called the kids. I gave them a full account of what was going on, and both seemed unusually quiet. I had previously informed them that this was going to happen soon, but did not want them to be with me when I had to leave David at Pine Haven. After promising to visit as soon as possible, they appeared to accept the situation. I realized that they had seen this coming even sooner than I had.

I went to David's bedroom and began picking out the things he would need in his new home. We had slept in separate rooms for some time. As I sorted through the underwear, socks, and handkerchiefs that I had laundered so many times, I had to go on a version of autopilot and not think too much. I was not at all prepared to experience all this emotion.

I packed up the items and filled a large carton to donate to the area mission headquarters. There were so many miscellaneous items, and after a few hours, I lost the ability to make any more decisions. I was glad to hear the doorbell so I could walk out of the room. The frantically barking dogs beat me to the door, and I had to confine them into the kitchen before opening it. I was glad to see my friend and neighbor, Rachel. She was carrying a small plate of fresh blueberry muffins.

"Kate," she said, "put the coffee on. Let's sit a while." I had told her I was taking David to see the doctor, and I suppose it was obvious to her that I would soon be returning alone. In recent months she had been the one person to whom I had turned. We sat at the kitchen table for a few minutes enjoying our muffins.

I told her the high points of what had happened, and she came over and gave me a hug. By now I knew I could ask almost anything of her. For years we had shared many life events. I sat at the hospital when her mother was dying of breast cancer. She had let Holly stay at her house for a couple of days when she was angry at us and threatening to run away. At age

8, my daughter decided to come back home quickly. We never talked about it again.

"Larry can mow your yard Saturday," Rachel said. He and David had been friends for a long time, also. In the past months, Larry had noticeably felt awkward about David's change, and they hadn't spent much time together.

I knew I could depend on Rachel, but for today, I told her I just wanted to be alone for a bit. She gave me another quick embrace and left.

Over the next few weeks I slowly returned to my normal routine and chores while trying to take care of all the things on the list. I met with the lawyer and signed the necessary papers giving me total power of attorney. David and I had signed so many legal papers that I didn't think all that much about a few more. I finally visited him, and found his demeanor to be peaceful, the ever-present anger gone. He barely changed his expression when I walked into his room. It was then I found out that using various meds was frequently the accepted solution for managing the patients.

I also discovered his future needs would be very simple. About this time I came to the obvious realization that he wasn't just in rehab, recovering from something temporary. We as human beings are sometimes slow to accept situations. Call it hope, or fear of change, or whistling in the dark, or just hiding from the truth — it is hard to accept a dead-end road. How many times do we turn our car down a street clearly marked "NO EXIT," just to see for sure? Even when we are forced to make a U-turn, we are still shaking our heads in disbelief.

On the day I was forced to believe David would never return home, I made that U-turn.

CHAPTER TEN

When I did not see Grace the next day after I returned to the hospital, I was disappointed. Before I had begun to tell her the long tale, I dreaded going there. Even though David had only been there for a couple of days, it was a trying experience for me. I had to admit to myself now that finishing the telling of the story was the real reason I was there. David didn't even know me, as usual, and it was only a sense of duty that made me check in on his progress. Somebody had to be there to see what the doctor had to say after his daily rounds. There wasn't much to report. They were closely monitoring the circulation in David's leg and he needed to stay for a few more days. I am sure our excellent insurance made this an easy decision.

I took a seat in the solarium with a hot cup of coffee and picked up a magazine. The temperature was supposed to take a big drop by evening, so I was planning to leave soon. I was startled when my cell phone rang. I didn't really get many calls any more. My children called in the evenings, and many of my friends had drifted away. Even loyal friends do not feel comfortable asking about this type of ongoing situation. I remembered how so many of them had struggled to figure out what to say. Rachel had been my best friend for years, and our families had shared so much, but after I moved out of the neighborhood we didn't see each other all that much. Daily conversations had turned into an occasional phone call.

I fumbled for the phone, which had fallen to the bottom of my handbag. I did not recognize the number but soon found it to be Grace.

"Honey, I wanted to let you know our son has been released, so we won't be at the hospital anymore."

I felt a huge pang of disappointment but tried to keep my voice level. She went on to say that she and Jack really wanted me to visit their small apartment in a nearby retirement community. I was so glad I had given her my phone number.

I thanked her and said. "Grace, you don't know how much this means to me. I would have hated not knowing why you weren't here. I can come by anytime you wish."

She asked if I was free later that very afternoon, and I was soon smiling and making plans to spend a few more hours with the enchanting couple. Grace did most of the talking for both her and Jack, but I could always see approval in her spouse's eyes. I was pretty sure that anything making his wife happy was priority to him.

My favorite bakery was on the way, so I made a quick stop for some of their delicious muffins. It wasn't long before I turned into the long driveway at the facility where they lived. It was a large place with choices for tenants to make. One building only provided housekeeping assistance, while another provided more medical care.

The place that David now lived in was much different. Although it was discreet, there was limited access. Some of the patients had the tendency to wander away, while others became a danger to themselves and others despite taking medication.

I drove down the winding drive around a lake which had several geese around it. It was beautifully landscaped and currently decorated with fall flowers. The November chill was definitely in the air, and I tightened the orange scarf close around my neck as I got out of the car, then started looking for the apartment number I had written down.

I knocked at the door, and Grace called for me to come in. She was sitting on a floral chair with her feet propped up on a footstool. It was a small space with only the main room, a tiny kitchen, and a bedroom with attached bath. Jack was watching television in the bedroom. I showed her the muffins, and offered to make some coffee.

"Oh, honey, that was so thoughtful of you!" she said. "I don't worry about those carbs anymore." She told me where to find cups, spoons, and cream and sugar. I spotted some small paper plates, and took them to the table near where she was sitting.

We made small talk about the weather, how her son was adapting to new eating habits, and the usual subjects of polite conversation. Grace stopped talking and gave me a look like she was expecting something more.

She could stand it no longer and said, "Please continue the story."

CHAPTER ELEVEN

Grace brushed a few muffin crumbs from her lap and settled back, eager to hear more of my story. Her bright blue eyes told me how much she was enjoying this. I quickly gave her a summary of how David had needed to live at Pine Haven, and the changes in my life that had come about. I could not bring myself to think too much about this recent past right now. It was a lot easier to go much further back.

I stood, walked to the window, and pulled aside the lace curtains to look out. I always hated the time of the year when it gets dark earlier and earlier. As I peered out into the gathering twilight, I told Grace it would soon be time for me to go. She and Jack would head to the facility's dining room for their evening meal.

Impulsively, she asked where I was going for Thanksgiving, and I realized it was only a few days away. I wasn't sure what was going on with my children yet, so I told Grace I would get back to her. Thanking her for the invitation, I turned and said, "Don't worry; you are not getting rid of me easily now!" I had actually come to adore the little lady, and hoped to see her from time to time.

"Is there a lot more to tell?" she asked.

"You will not believe how much more there is," I replied with a shake of my head.

By the time I was settling into the car, a chilly rain had begun. I hated to get out again, but there wasn't much food in my kitchen. I pulled into a brightly lit grocery parking lot. I still feared being out alone at night.

A bowl of soup with some crusty French bread sounded inviting. I headed for the deli and asked the attendant what the soup of the day was, planning on chicken noodle. She told me that they had the most delicious homemade mushroom soup I would ever eat. I threw back my head and laughed as the puzzled young woman looked on. I quickly apologized and bought a large container of chicken noodle soup, a loaf of bread, and grabbed a pint of rum raisin ice cream at the last minute. I spied a colorful bouquet of autumn mums and splurged on those, as well.

I was still smiling when I got into the car to drive home.

After eating supper I reached for the remote to turn on the television. I really needed to stop thinking about so many different aspects of the past. I flipped through the channels and settled on a familiar movie. The centerpiece of mums in my antique crystal vase made the room seem much more cheerful.

Most of the photos from the last few decades were stored on my laptop, but my eyes wandered to the cabinet that held the older albums. I took out a few of the thick ones and started flipping through them. These familiar images were frozen memories of all those long past days. With the holidays now fast approaching, I allowed myself to wallow in the pain of seeing the happy years.

My children were wide-eyed babies happily unwrapping dolls, toys, and so much more. Both the grandmothers were still alive, and David looked young and strong. I chuckled at my own images, with big dark hair and clothing that reflected all the trends of that time, including shoulder pads and mini-skirts.

My son Eric was grinning, holding up a new sweatshirt with the logo of his favorite team. Holly was still an innocent toddler, holding a new doll. Where had those years gone? I gazed at the old photographs for a long time, as though I could jump back into them.

Eric had lived through an insane first wife and now had his hands full with his own children and job. His second wife, Ellie, was a good mother, and I was glad she would be there to take care of him as they aged. Until recently, I hadn't realized how important this was.

The digital photos of more recent holidays were even more difficult to see. The grandmothers were gone, and it was bitter-sweet to see my children in previous relationships. I saw all the thoughtful gifts I had carefully chosen for people who did not deserve them.

However, the worst ones were taken recently when David was not himself, and eventually no longer home. That first year we tried to bring him home for the holidays, but it took both children to assist me in taking him back. In the past year, we had just visited a man who did not know us.

I used to love the holidays, decorating every room. I baked and cooked an abundance of food, which we often ended up wasting.

I remembered those happy years when Holly was a teenager and we decorated cookies together. Even though she will be coming home for a few days this year, she and her husband will have other people to visit and it will go by quickly.

The prospect of seeing the decorations at David's facility, lighting up things for residents and visitors, only seemed very sad for me. When I put a small tree in his room that first year he became upset and more confused. I didn't do it again.

I chided myself for being so depressed because several of those strong women who had come before me suffered through worse holidays.

My mother, Victoria, remembered Grandmother Belle telling what she remembered of her childhood Christmases while the Civil War was going on. The men were off fighting, and those were lean years with only small gifts. The year after her older brother was killed at Gettysburg there was little joy, only bitter tears. She was only a child for most of that time, but the stories had been re-told so many times Belle felt she was actually remembering it. Even after they relocated to Illinois most holidays were bittersweet. For Southerners, the tragic War years had taken a toll that could not be forgotten.

Money was always scarce when Belle was raising her own children. She worked hard all her life, and after she was consumed with guilt over the death of Frances' baby, there wasn't much happiness for years. That first Christmas after Aaron's tragic death must have been horrible for Henry and Frances. Of course, my poor little mother must have felt confused and sad, too. Later, during World War II, I'm sure Frances worried herself into a terrible state as her spoiled Jesse was fighting in North Africa.

CHAPTER TWELVE

I was very happy when Eric dropped by the next day. Unlike Holly, he didn't live all that far away. However, I knew he had his hands full with work, children, and other responsibilities. Especially since David was no longer the grandfather they remembered from earlier years, I only saw my grandchildren occasionally.

I still saw a shy little boy when I looked at my son, not the middle-aged man with a frown and prematurely receding hairline. I tried not to be a burden on either of my children, and that resolve was the driving force when I sold the big home I sorely missed.

Soon after the auction I was moved into this place. I had a difficult time letting go of so many items I had dearly loved for so long. The kids had been allowed to pick out anything they wanted to keep, but it was disappointing when they didn't want to become the next custodians of all the family things.

Eric gave me a hug, asked about David, and sat down at the table. He wasn't a coffee drinker and declined anything. I knew him enough to realize he had something to tell me, but was trying to find the right words.

"Eric," I said, "What's up?"

"Mom, you know I hate to disappoint you, but we have to

go to Chicago for Thanksgiving. My in-laws really want to see the kids, and we haven't been there in a while. I hate to leave you alone, with dad and all, but I have to do this."

He paused, waiting for me to object, but those years were long behind me. It had taken me a long time to realize that the festive holiday years when the kids were growing up were long behind me, never to return. I resisted pointing out that I was nearby, but also rarely saw the children any more.

So, I only said, "Eric, I understand. I actually have an invitation for Thanksgiving, so all is well."

A look of relief came over his face. It felt good to take one worry off his mind. His first wife had been a huge disappointment and source of stress, and I was happy his life had taken a turn for the better. Even I hadn't realized she was suffering from a form of mental illness until it was way too late.

Looking back it was obvious, but she was gone now, their marriage just another memory. I heard she was living in West Virginia with her sixth husband. The greatest blessing was that she and Eric hadn't had children.

Eric and I discussed other topics — how the children were doing, his work, and of course, David. I knew Eric could not bear to see his father as a stranger who didn't recognize him, so he rarely went to visit anymore.

Months ago, I had reassured him it was okay. David's main caretaker had confided to me that many folks there did not see any family members for long stretches of time. This cruel illness is simply heartbreaking. The person they loved has disappeared, and it is very hard to relate to the change.

Just before I had begun to suspect that David was changing, we had lost a very important family friend. He and David were buddies for a long time. It was very hard for him to watch his pal slowly be defeated by cancer, coupled with the horrific chemo and radiation that only tortured him in his last days. I had to wonder which was the worse way to meet one's last days on Earth.

When we had two big black Labradors we didn't let them suffer when it was apparent only pain was in their immediate future. I've never figured out why we're allowed to treat our pets more humanely than fellow humans.

I insisted Eric take a bag of treats with him when he left. I have always baked a particular type of chocolate chip and oatmeal cookies just for him.

Suddenly the house seemed very empty. It has always been hard for me to watch one of my children leave. Two furry faces quickly reminded me it was time for their supper. I then fixed a small meal for myself and settled in for the evening.

It wasn't long before I reached for the phone and entered Grace's number. When she answered, I told her that I would be excited to join her for Thanksgiving. We would be going to the lavish banquet room at the facility where she and Jack lived, and I was looking forward to meeting some of her family. I inquired about bringing along a dish of some type, and found myself smiling.

I slept well that night, but awoke thinking about some Thanksgivings of the past. I tried to be thankful I had all of those wonderful years to remember. I recalled the enormous task that it had been to pull those meals together. I always managed to get several spots of turkey grease on my shirt and burn a few fingers. When we would get out the "good dishes" and genuine silver flatware, everything seemed just as it should be.

I glanced over to the hutch, directing my gaze to the violet-covered tureen, and marveled at how it had survived for so long. It used to hold gravy at Thanksgiving.

CHAPTER THIRTEEN

For the past few years I hadn't done much about Thanksgiving. The years of well-planned dinners, lots of guests, and a real holiday feeling were long gone. I remembered how I used to complain about the mess of baking a turkey, with lots of greasy pans to wash and the chore of picking the meat off the carcass. I had inherited a gaudy turkey platter from David's mother, and it became tradition to use it every year. After many car trips and washings, the heirloom had sold at the big auction for only a dollar. As I watched it walk away, I felt memories leave with it.

David and I had often gone out to eat Thanksgiving dinner at a nice restaurant. Last year I ate a hasty meal in the Pine Haven cafeteria. The obviously once-frozen pumpkin pie was topped with a dollop of whipped topping from a can. It only reminded me of much better pies from long ago.

I actually decided to bake a sweet potato pie from a family recipe to take to Grace's family gathering. I also made a frozen creamy Jell-O dessert I hadn't thought of in years.

Holly called to express her regret she could not be with me, and told of their plans to eat at a fancy restaurant with some of her co-workers. We made small talk for a few minutes, I told her how much I loved her, and we said good-bye.

On Thanksgiving morning the skies were bright blue even though it was cold — an uplifting sight as I drove across town. Grace and Jack reserved the party room in their assisted living complex and arranged for much of the dinner to be prepared by the staff. However, to make the holiday seem less institutional, their family was supplying other parts of the meal.

I was introduced to those in attendance, all of whom made me feel welcome and at ease. I always felt people should dress up for holidays, and wore a black beaded sweater with crisp, cream woolen pants, along with my gold jewelry. I was hardly surprised to notice that many of the younger folks were in jeans and t-shirts. This was another change that had taken me a while to accept.

I made polite conservation while we ate. It was good to feel like I was part of a family again, even one that was not my own. These days people have the tendency to eat and run, just saying a quick thanks before leaving. Everyone is always in a hurry with other places to be, perhaps another branch of the family to visit. The Thanksgivings I remember fondly lasted all day, starting with the ladies cooking and laughing while the men watched television. The meal itself was slow paced, ending with dessert and coffee. It took several hours for the dishes to be washed and put away, being very careful of the "good" china. Sometimes games were played or several of us went on a walk around the neighborhood. It was usually after dark before anyone left. We never considered future Thanksgivings would be so different.

I could tell by the look on Grace's face she was thinking the very same thing. By 4 p.m., everyone had gone. I retrieved the dishes that had held the pie and salad and was thinking of leaving also. Grace turned to me with a pleading look and said, "Oh, please, can you come to our apartment and stay a while longer? I hate it when these things are over so soon!"

I was only too happy to agree. I had looked in on David

earlier in the day, and felt no guilt about not going back. I put my dishes in the car and drove the short distance to their apartment. By now they were tired, and Jack soon left us for a nap. We settled into the cozy living room and chatted for a few minutes. Grace told me how Jack had proposed to her all of those years ago, and laughed as she remembered how he had been red-faced and flustered. I recognized the look that came over her when she talked about the man she had loved for so very long.

She turned to me and asked about my "courtship" with David. I hesitated for a moment. I wanted to believe I could tell this story in an accurate way.

"Well, Grace, I never stopped wondering why my father abandoned my mother and I. Even as a young adult, this deep need was always in my subconscious. David, being my former professor, was like a father figure to me, I suppose."

CHAPTER FOURTEEN

Grace was listening with the same interested look she always had when I told her these stories. I think I was becoming like the live version of a new soap opera to her.

I kind of paused right there, and she asked if I wanted coffee and more of the leftover pie. For so many years I had avoided calorie-laden holiday desserts, but I suddenly decided more pie would be the perfect way to end the day. It was already dark outside and I thought I should be going.

Between bites I started talking again, so the story continued.

"I never really knew David all that well when he was my professor, and we didn't seem to have much in common. We met again by accident a few years later and began to see each other. It was not expected, and sometimes I have to think our lives are decided by chance."

"Grace, by the time that David and I re-connected as adults, I was so needy for love and comfort that it wasn't long before I felt ready to have a physical relationship with this man. I assumed he had been in other affairs with many women, so it wasn't anything that made much of a difference to him. But I felt it was a commitment, an unspoken agreement. I had found someone to take care of me."

"My greatest fear in life was being abandoned, discarded,

and unloved. I vowed to myself to do all that I could to not let this happen again. From sex to accepting some of his friends, I went along with it all. Even when he was over an hour late to pick me up for a date, I kept silent."

"Did you continue to go to college?" asked Grace. "What did you do all day?"

"No, at that time I had a job, even though it was nothing like the important career I had foreseen for myself. Looking back, I think I must have had a sort of mental lapse for a few years, because I made so many sudden decisions. I went to work in a small real estate office. I can't even remember a lot of those months."

"Looking back now, I can see myself doing things, but it is like watching someone else. I began to argue with my mother about spending all of my time with David. I'm sure she did not recognize this different person I had become."

"It didn't take Mom long to realize I was sleeping with him because I would spend entire weekends in his seedy apartment. We went out with other couples — his friends — most of whom I had nothing in common with. David was used to living the party life and expected me to fit in."

"When we weren't at his place we parked behind a rural church. He used to laugh about the little old ladies coming to worship on Sunday morning and finding the used condoms he had thrown out of the car window the night before."

"The community still thought of him as the cool, young professor, and we had that image as a couple. I ignored everything I did not really feel right about because I wasn't alone anymore and I liked the position of being David's girlfriend. By now, I was in love with him anyway, and considered him my lover, my protector, and my future."

Grace was yawning so I offered to go, but she begged me to tell more. This part of the story was the "juicy part," she said. We could hear Jack snoring loudly from the bedroom.

"Grace, I grew up watching the lifelong love affair between my grandparents, Henry and Frances. My grandmother was a difficult person much of the time, but Henry never wavered. He was always there to hold her hand, put his arm around her, and help her — even when he was sick himself. I don't recall hearing him speak loudly to her. He worshipped that tiny French woman and I just assumed all marriages were like this."

"It didn't take me long to notice this was not the way of David Williams. He was always showing this brashness, but even that seemed exciting to me. In the late summer of that year, he and an old college friend went on a trip. I went to work as usual. I felt left out, jealous. He called a few times and sent postcards. I wish I could remember what was said on his last call to me before coming home. At the end of that conversation, we had somehow decided to get married. We simply got up and eloped to another state, with my mother not finding out until later."

I paused here. Grace had a totally shocked look on her face. She tried to speak but words failed her. I realized that both the day and the story should end here. She agreed, and I hugged her before heading out into the dark night. I threw my bright green scarf around my neck and shivered. Winter was coming early.

CHAPTER FIFTEEN

As I drove home on that chilly evening I saw people already waiting for various stores to open and allow them to race in. For years, shopping on "Black Friday" had been a yearly tradition. The stores seemed to open earlier every year. I hated this trend and never went, even when I was younger. Christmas shopping was one of the many things that had changed dramatically over the course of my life. I tried to resist those thoughts crowding into my mind, but they came to me, anyway.

When David and I were first married Christmas gift money was in short supply, so I shopped very carefully. Many of the gifts we gave were either handmade or inexpensive. Much later, when it was fairly easy to spend lots more, the concept was not nearly as magical.

My children once eagerly awaited unwrapping small gifts like new crayons, games, and even clothing. But as years passed, Christmas lost the feeling I had always known. During the last decade or so in the big house I continued to decorate, but I no longer had the enthusiasm of the lean years.

My grandchildren send me a "want list" that I tried to shop from each year when they were younger, but after they became teenagers I just bought gift cards. It became increasingly difficult for me to find the spirit of Christmas.

On this drive home I let down my usual defenses. I was sobbing by the time I arrived back at the house. The sweet doggies had been alone for hours, so they greeted me with accusing looks and a lot of barking. I have a nice neighbor who let them out in the yard while I was gone. Susan looked forward to my calls requesting help. I tried to visit with her whenever I could, understanding only too well what it was like to be alone.

Susan had worked for many years at one of the large chain stores. She had lost her husband quite a few years before, and her children lived far away. She was part of a group of ladies that often got together, and they had asked me to join them several times. Tonight, I noticed a small Christmas tree was already lit up in her front window.

I settled into my chair after attending to the dogs, and then took down a few albums of photos from early in our marriage. That first Christmas was another that I would like to forget, but I forced myself to view the blurry photos and remember. My mother had not taken the news of our sudden marriage very well, and for months, she would not even take my phone calls.

I am sure most couples do not start off their life together by arguing all night, as David and I did. Many times, I got up and went to work without sleeping at all. I was then still young enough to believe that life was like 1950s television, and if one figured out how to explain a situation the other person understood. I am not even sure what we really argued about, but it always ended the same. Nothing was resolved, and life just went on.

In one photo I saw the sparse white pine Christmas tree we had that first Christmas. It was decorated with only a few ornaments and a smattering of tinsel. We had gone into Uncle Jesse's woods and cut it down ourselves. He and his wife seemed to revel in the knowledge I had a major divide in the relationship with my mother, and they did all that they could to support David and I. Many weekends they would invite us to their house to eat two-inch thick steaks and play cards. It was years down the road before I realized all of this was only to snub his sister.

It wasn't enough to have always been Frances' favorite — Jesse had to twist the knife. Before I was married to David, they never gave me the time of day and criticized everything I did. I can remember Jesse saying he thought I was a "bad bet."

Of course, David enjoyed being treated like a prince, so he was always ready to go to their house. Jesse loved to tell stories about me as a child to make me look stupid or naughty. All three people would then look at me and laugh. By now, I started to realize my rash decision to run off and get married was not without consequences.

My mother had always been my buddy, the one person who was there for me. If only she had not chosen to cut me out of her life, maybe things would have gone in another direction. I went out that first Christmas, bought her a nice blouse, and headed to her home to give it to her. She was actually driving away when I got there, but I flagged her down and attempted to give her the gift. I was foolishly thinking this would repair everything. Instead, she grabbed it out of my hands, threw the carefully wrapped box onto the highway, and drove away.

I stood there in the middle of the road staring at the ruined package long after the sound of her squealing tires faded away. The pretty blouse had spilled out, and it was a sight I would never forget. If I ever had any doubts, I now knew there would be no backing up. I had no life to return to, so I must make everything work. It would be years before I could see how my mother had spent much of her life in emotional pain. It was even longer before I could see I was expecting David to magically become the ideal type of man I had envisioned for myself.

One day right before that Christmas, David brought home a square box, threw it under our tree, and turned to me. "There." he said. "If you want to complain and think I don't love you, just open that." Without another word, he spun around and left.

When I was sure he was gone, I actually did open it, carefully peeling back the Scotch tape from the red foil. Inside I found a small diamond ring — the engagement ring I had never received. I carefully re-wrapped it. When Christmas came, I had the task of really opening the gift. It was the first of hundreds of award-winning performances.

Yes, this was a bittersweet Christmas memory. As I stared at the photos of a young couple with haircuts and clothing of the 60s, now knowing all they would face, I wept.

CHAPTER SIXTEEN

When my phone rang on Saturday, I wasn't surprised to see it was Grace calling me. I quickly thanked her again for making my Thanksgiving Day so much better than it would have been. We made small talk, and then Grace said, "Honey, I hope you won't think this is too personal for me to ask, but I was wondering which church you attend."

I was not expecting that question, so it took me a few seconds to reply.

"Well, Grace, I'll have to admit I haven't gone to church in years. David never had any interest in going. He had way too much church forced on him as a child so he avoided organized religion after that."

I went on to say I had attended a small church as a child, but it was easy for me to find a personal way to understand the meaning of life without it. I tried to explain myself without insulting whatever Grace and Jack might believe. Talking about politics or religion is always a slippery slope.

Grace and Jack attended church right there at the senior complex, and she wanted to know if I might want to go with them. I realized this amazing lady sensed it might make the upcoming holiday season more bearable for me.

I quickly considered my options when Grace asked me to

go to their services. With the approaching holidays I decided this might be a way to find some happiness and peace. After all, this should come from inside every person and not depend on anything said or done by others.

"Grace," I replied, "thanks for thinking of me. That would definitely brighten up Christmas for me this year. Just let me know when and where I should go."

I could almost see her face light up. "Well, honey, they put up the holiday greenery right after Thanksgiving, and that is my favorite time of the year."

Before I knew it, I had agreed to meet them at the church Sunday morning. I started thinking about what to wear, which took me right back to childhood. I remembered being in Christmas programs and going to practice for them. People of all ages met at the church on Saturday afternoons to be assigned small speaking parts and learn the old hymns.

I now thought of this time as the part of my life with the most continuity and purpose. These simple programs brought people together to make Christmas what it should be. I am pretty sure that bigotry, ignorance, and intolerance was not included at that church.

I smiled as I thought of the importance of having a beautiful dress to wear. One that stands out in my memory was a shirtwaist made of red brocade, worn with a couple of crinolines underneath. I closed my eyes and sighed. This season used to make everyone forget all the world's ugly parts.

I knew those days and my youth would never return, but perhaps I could find something to anchor my happiness and sanity to this new reality that faced me.

I suddenly realized a part of me had changed since the day I encountered Grace and Jack in the hospital waiting room a few weeks ago. I no longer really remembered why I had started telling Grace the story of all that had happened. For decades I had said and done what was necessary to make my life stay on course. It was like being in a perpetual play, being fed the proper lines and actions on a teleprompter.

A long line of women in my family had played out similar lives. From the time of Belle and even her mother, it was necessary to keep smiling and ignore the rest.

The story of the tureen came to mind. I knew it was time to tell Holly this long-held family secret. I had always avoided this because I wasn't sure if she would understand. I was also unsure of how accurate the information really was. Holly was a realist and expressed disbelief and skepticism about many things. I secretly wished I could be more capable of thinking this way.

Perhaps if Grandma Frances had been in a closer relationship with my poor mother, she would have told her. But no, she decided I was the one better suited to understand. There is no doubt in my mind this was a wise decision. I was sixteen years old on the snowy afternoon when we had this conversation. Frances was sitting in the maple chair wearing her ever-present calico dress and home-sewn apron. I was at the oak dining table, trying to get the ancient typewriter to work.

I will never know why she chose that afternoon.

CHAPTER SEVENTEEN

T he church service I had attended with Grace was still on my mind as the holidays approached. Jack, as usual, was tired and did not go with us. I was only too happy to patiently help Grace settle into the front seat of my car and carefully stow her walker in the trunk. Her church had a ramp to accommodate handicapped members. Even though it was located on the campus of the senior facility, it was far enough away that driving around the large loop was the easiest way to get there.

The experience was moving and I found more comfort than expected. The Christmas hymns really seemed to ease my turbulent thoughts. It actually made me decide not to tell Grace my whole story that day. I took her back to her residence and found myself actually smiling. I was very used to putting on a false smile just like my clothing every day. I had been doing it for so long it came naturally now.

However, on that morning, just a few weeks before Christmas, I realized true peace and happiness was closer to me than it had been in a long time. I went through the holiday season with a lighter heart than I had for several years. Even when I visited David's room, which was, of course, expected, I felt a wave of compassion for this man who was trapped inside a body and mind that was no longer his younger self.

The usual long-standing feeling of being trapped in this part of my life wasn't as bitter to me. I sat with him, seeing his vacant stare for a few hours on Christmas Eve, then walked down the long hall to the elevators, feeling still very alone.

When I entered the elevator that led to the parking garage, the doors opened briefly on another floor. A man wearing a white doctor's coat stepped in. He was an older man with a neatly trimmed salt and pepper beard who carried a coat over his arm.

I assumed he had been called to another patient's room and wondered if someone had experienced a crisis, or even passed away. Since I had gotten to know many of the other residents and their families, I decided to ask. This pleasant-looking doctor seemed to be the kind of person I felt comfortable speaking to.

"Excuse me, sir, but I have to wonder if you had to come here tonight because someone had a problem. I am sorry for asking, but I know some of them."

I went on to say that my husband was in a room on an upper floor, and found myself talking way too much, as usual.

The friendly-looking man gave me an understanding look, and explained that he was also here just to visit. He gave me a little smile, and went on to say his wife was also a resident and had been for a while.

He then realized I had been looking at his doctor's coat with a puzzled look.

"Oh, I forgot I was wearing this. I came straight from the hospital. I am kind of retired, but still work part time. It is just too quiet at my house, and I love to help people. I always volunteer to work part of Christmas Eve — that lets the young guys with families go home."

"My name is Gordon, Gordon Livingston. And yes, I have heard the old 'Dr. Livingston, I presume' joke a million times. That really is my name and I am a doctor!"

I stammered out my name and put out my hand to shake his. No one would ever call Dr. Livingston a handsome man, but his personality made up for his looks. He wasn't all that tall and could stand to lose a few pounds, but the smile coming out of his eyes made him seem like a person who would naturally draw people to him.

He asked in a very sincere way about David, and I suddenly noticed we had emerged from the elevator and were walking along together toward the parking area.

"Oh, I am sorry," I said, "I did not mean to hold you up. I'm sure you have had a long evening and want to get out of here."

"No, no," he said, "I am never in a hurry to get home any more, especially on Christmas Eve. Would you like to get a cup of coffee?"

The indecision must have showed on my face, so he continued. "No worries, I have no ulterior motives here. When I was a lot younger I might have just wanted to pick up a pretty girl, but these days I am just badly in need of another human being to have a conversation with. My son lives on the other side of the country. Even though he will call tomorrow morning, I am on my own tonight."

A few minutes later I found myself getting into the passenger seat of his car. Gordon said he'd bring me back to mine later. For a doctor, he drove an older model sedan, so I assumed that perhaps his wife's healthcare had depleted his savings.

I felt I had discovered a kindred spirit when he had to throw some junk mail and newspapers from the passenger seat to the back, just like I usually did. David always made a sarcastic remark when I repeated this action over the years.

There was an all-night coffee shop a few blocks away. I was surprised when Gordon ran around and opened my car door. Nobody had done that for a very long time.

"They know me here," he smiled, "I often stop by on my way home."

A young waitress greeted us with a big grin. "Merry Christmas, Dr. Livingston," she said. "I was hoping you would stop by. Hang on a minute." She reached behind the counter and returned with a brightly colored tin.

"I baked you these cookies, so I am glad I was able to give them to you."

Gordon jumped up from his seat in our booth and gave her a big hug. "Lindsay, you are too good to an old man. This is my new friend, Kate, and we just wanted to have a quick cup of that excellent coffee."

Lindsay returned with two steaming mugs of decaf. We had laughed when we both asked for the same.

Gordon told me he used to drink as much regular coffee as he could to get him through the long hospital hours, but he swiftly switched after retirement.

"After realizing I could actually get the sleep I was deprived of for all of those years, I found I no longer wanted to be too wired to sleep. Today I only drink caffeine in the early morning."

"Now," he said, "Tell me your story."

I did not tell him the much longer version as I had told Grace, but it still took me a while to even relate the main facts. Lindsay had already re-filled our cups, and we had eaten a few cookies from the tin.

Gordon thoughtfully listened without interrupting, but a look of understanding and compassion had come over his face.

"Well, I have been living this lifestyle for a bit longer. My wife, Mary Anne, was in a car accident on a snowy evening four years ago. She isn't brain dead, so there was no big quality of life decision to make, but she never regained any memory of her previous life. She is also paralyzed from the waist down. Being in a safe place where she could get 24-hour care was the only option."

"For a long time," he continued, "she wanted nothing to do with me. I was a stranger to her. I kept believing she would start to remember, but it does not look like that will ever happen.

Gradually, we became just new friends, and I showed her photos of our life together. However, the new Mary Anne was nothing like the girl I had fallen in love with all those years ago. Our son moved far away because it was too painful to visit a mother who did not know him. At least once a year, I fly out to visit him and his family, and I Skype with the grandkids, but he won't come back here. I understand that."

I glanced at my watch and realized it was almost 1 a.m.

"Merry Christmas!" I said to Gordon. "We have been sitting here a long time."

He left Lindsay a generous tip, wished her Merry Christmas, and we left. It had gotten sharply colder and I pulled my coat collar up a bit higher. Gordon reached out to help, but immediately apologized.

"Oh, sorry, I did that so often for Mary Anne. It just came back to me."

I smiled and told him how nice it was to have someone who actually cared whether I was cold or not. On the short drive back to where my car was parked, we had fallen into silence. I guessed we were both wondering how to end the evening.

After pulling up alongside my vehicle, Gordon reached into his inside coat pocket and pulled out a business card. He laughed and said he had a lifetime supply of these, so he gave them out to anyone he happened to get to know.

"It is just my office number," he said. "I don't usually give out personal information, but hang on."

He pulled out a pen and scribbled his cell phone number on the back.

"Call me any time," he smiled. "I have enjoyed this evening."

"Well, Gordon, you spared me from a lonely Christmas Eve, too."

I took out a little notebook, quickly wrote my number on a page, then ripped it out and gave it to him.

After getting into my cold car, I couldn't help but wave as I drove away. I hadn't enjoyed the company of a man for such a long time. I felt like a teenager on her first date.

However, I had barely driven a couple of blocks before reality began to sink in. This kind doctor had only been looking for a pleasant way to soften this quiet holiday evening. This was just a chance encounter and it was unlikely we would ever see each other again.

I found myself feeling as if a heaviness had begun to lift from my heart and perhaps there was still more to the rest of my life than I had dared to hope.

As New Year's Eve approached I found myself feeling guilty about wishing it could be spent with Gordon. However, after paying a short visit to David, I went home alone. I told myself I was a foolish woman, reading more into those few hours in the coffee shop than I should have.

On the following morning my phone rang and I sprinted to answer it, hoping to hear the doctor's mellow voice. However, it was Grace.

"Where have you been?" she said. "I didn't want to be a bother, but it's been several days since I've heard from you. Is everything okay?"

"Oh, I had a cold over Christmas," I quickly lied, "and I didn't want to bring you germs."

"Oh, honey, that is okay, but I sure did miss talking to you. I seem to remember that you had something important to tell me."

I had nearly forgotten that.

CHAPTER EIGHTEEN

I wrestled with indecision. It hadn't been all that long ago I had made a firm plan to be totally open with Grace. I had also toyed with the idea of telling Holly. Both possibilities now seemed wrong. It is tiring to keep family secrets, especially for as long as I had. I thought back to the afternoon I had listened to Grandma Frances share the history of how it all began. I wondered how she knew it was possible to tell me and be sure of my reaction. That was uppermost in my mind on a chilly morning in mid-January when my phone rang.

I had been avoiding having a long conversation with Grace for a few weeks now, and I expected to hear her voice when I answered the phone. By now, I had mostly given up on hearing from Gordon, so it was a pleasant surprise to hear his voice.

"Kate," he said, "I would not be surprised if you never wanted to speak to me ever again. It has been very rude of me to not call with an explanation. Do you remember that I told you I was expecting my son to call on Christmas Day? Well, he did call and told me he wanted to surprise me with a trip to see him. I was instructed to pack quickly because there was an airplane ticket waiting for me at the terminal. I did just that, and barely made it in time."

"I had steeled myself to having a lonely day, and it was a

delightful gift. Unfortunately, I was barely on the plane before I realized I had left my cell phone at home on the charger. Not only was I without a phone, but all of my contacts were in its memory. I wanted to call you but there was no way to do so."

"My son insisted I stay and visit with him and his family for a few weeks, so I did just that. He knew how to contact the care facility when Mary Anne is, and we could explain my absence to them. I should have asked them to give you a message, but it just did not occur to me to do so."

I had remained silent while listening to his explanation and felt a swift lifting of a weight off my mind. I hadn't even recognized how important Gordon had already become to me. I felt guilty about the smile that had spread over my face. Despite all that had gone on with David, I felt the responsibility of being his totally faithful wife. Even before his illness had progressed we hadn't had the best relationship. However, I had long ago resolved to handle it with as much honor as possible.

"Oh, that is okay — I totally understand. I had wondered a bit, though," I said. "I was afraid something bad had happened."

I could almost picture the twinkle in Gordon's eyes as he spoke.

"I would really like to make it up to you," he said. "Can I take you out to dinner?"

He must have sensed I was pausing to think this over, because he quickly went on.

"I told my son about running into you and explained how nice it was for me to have a kindred soul to speak with. He loves his mother deeply, but understood my need for human companionship. I had feared he might not think it right for me to enjoy the company of another woman. It is a devastating thing to see Mary Anne wither away. If you recall, that is why he felt the need to move so far away."

I felt it was my turn to say something.

"The situation with David is very different, but with similar truths. I go to visit, but I know that he has no idea if I am his wife or just another annoying nurse. Like Mary Anne, he sees a stranger standing there."

"It is a sad situation for all of us," Gordon said. "In so many ways, all four of us do not have a life anymore."

"So," he went on to say, "please have dinner with me. We are at sea in lifeboats not of our making. I don't want to keep coming home to a silent house. One of these days I really will have to retire, and my days as a doctor will be at an end. I don't know what I will do then. Unlike many of my fellow physicians, I do not play golf and I detest spending time at the country club. I am happy that Mary Anne and I did a lot of traveling through the years, because I have no heart to do so alone now."

"Gordon," I found myself saying, "I would be happy to join you for dinner. I will look forward to it."

A plan was quickly made. Gordon said that he would pick me up on the following Saturday evening.

After hanging up, I literally just sat there with a crooked little smile on my face, sorting out several thoughts. I immediately wanted to talk to Grace now. I had to tell someone else. I felt like a teenager going out on a date, and this thought made laugh out loud. My next thoughts went to wondering what to wear.

I reached out and grabbed the phone. I tapped out Grace's number then impatiently waited for her to answer. When she was on the line, I took a deep breath and tried not to sound too excited. I first apologized for not being in touch, but then asked if I could come for a visit. She sounded happy to hear my voice.

"Kate, of course you can come for a visit. Why don't you join us for lunch?"

On the way to their apartment, I realized how much I wanted her blessing to go out with Gordon. I also thought this would make the perfect excuse for my absence.

Grace answered the door wearing a lavender pantsuit with a floral scarf around her neck. For the months that I had known her, I had never seen her unkempt in any way. Down to her tiny feet, she always seemed perfect.

With a little laugh, she said she had just had her hair fixed and was hoping someone would see it. Like most senior living facilities, there was a beauty shop for the residents. They even arranged to pick up ladies who needed assistance with walking.

Jack was sitting on the couch, nodding off with the newspaper in his hand. Grace shook his arm, saying, "Come on, honey, Kate is here, so let's lunch in the dining room today." I knew that many times their meals were delivered, but they were always encouraged to go to the dining room if possible.

Jack jerked awake, slowly put his shoes on, and we started down to the dining room. This was a bright sunny day for midwinter and it was a pleasant place to eat with large windows and smiling attendants.

A surprisingly satisfying meal was brought to our table and we ate for a few minutes just making polite small talk. As always, Jack said very little, but Grace always made up for his silence. She told news of her family and how nice their holiday visits had been, showing off a new bracelet on her wrist that been a gift. We spoke of everything from the weather to various bits of news she had seen on television.

As Grace ate her little piece of cherry pie and sipped a second glass of tea, she turned to me and said, "Okay Kate, I can see you are just bursting to talk about something else. Is it David? Has he taken a turn? But, no, you don't seem concerned. Something has happened to make you happier than you have been since I met you. Tell me all about it."

I was amazed at how sharp this beautiful old lady was. She had the wit of a teenager and I was glad she was making it easy to tell about this latest development in my life. But before I could say a word, she struggled back to her feet and said we should go back to the apartment.

"Dear Jack has an afternoon show he likes to watch. He'll

do that in the bedroom, and we girls can have a nice long chat." Jack stood with a little smile then slowly followed his wife out of the dining hall.

Grace knew all the folks at other tables and spoke to each and every one. Even the sad sights of those deeply asleep in wheelchairs were not ignored. She gave each of them a gentle pat on the arm. A different section was reserved for those needing more care, but she went out of her way to connect with many of them.

Arriving back at their place, Jack gave her a knowing nod and went into the tiny bedroom, shutting the door behind him. I heard the television come on. Grace settled into her little chair and said, "Okay, tell me what's up."

CHAPTER NINETEEN

I had always thought I was good at keeping secrets. My fa-
cial expressions did not seem to give me away. But the fact
Grace had quickly figured out I had something big on my
mind made me rethink this. She asked me to make a pot of decaf coffee for us to share, and as I busied myself doing this she
peppered me with comments and questions.

I poured both of us mugs of coffee and settled into the chair
opposite her.

"Grace, I have come to think of you as family. I know you
will give me an honest opinion. I had a very interesting encounter on Christmas Eve. I know we have spoken a few times since
then, but I wasn't ready to talk about it yet." Thinking back to
the little white lie I had told her earlier in the month, I went on
to say that it was before I had gotten sick.

Starting at the beginning with my discouraging visit with
a vacant-eyed David, to stepping into the elevator, and all that
followed, I methodically related all that had happened.

While I spoke I tried to read her reactions. Although Grace
interrupted with a few questions from time to time, her expression remained impassive. By the time I had gotten to the part
about his recent phone call, I was already bracing for possible
disappointment in her opinion and advice. I did not want her

— or anyone else — to make me rethink having a dinner date with Gordon.

After I stopped talking there was an agonizingly long minute of silence.

The first words out of Grace's mouth were, "Honey, we have to go shopping. You must have something new to wear."

I was so relieved that she wasn't going to tell me not to go that I jumped up and hugged her tiny frame.

"Seriously honey, for as long as I have known you I have wanted to suggest how badly you need to refresh your wardrobe. There are many days you look a bit like a nun on vacation. It is high time you stop making yourself look older than me."

I had stopped looking for the latest fashion or anything exciting to wear. I just settled for what I thought was "classic," paired with sensible shoes. I did not really think it mattered much anymore. Much of my closet was well over ten years old. The outfit I had worn on Thanksgiving was one of the only dressy things I owned.

On the night I had encountered Gordon I had been wearing one of the Christmas sweaters I brought out each year. I remembered I had tied a red plaid scarf over my basic navy blue coat. This is the way he would be remembering me.

"Oh, my," I said to Grace, "you are so right. I have nothing to wear. Can you go shopping with me tomorrow morning?"

I could immediately tell this plan was exciting to the little woman.

However, I wanted to steer the conversation away from clothing. I bit my lip and took on a more serious tone.

"So Grace, you think it is okay for me to spend some time with him? I am certain he is a good man, even though we have only met this one time. I could just tell he wasn't a serial killer or anything. I felt totally safe from the first few minutes. As I told you, he is kind of in the same situation as I am and I think we can be of great help and comfort to each other."

When she went on to ask what he looked like, I struggled putting his description into words.

I laughed and said, "Well, I don't suppose I would make a very good witness to a crime, because I mainly remember his eyes. He was wearing his white doctor's coat, so I have no idea how he dresses otherwise. He is just kind of average, I guess. He actually looks like a doctor, I think. Maybe this is the reason I trusted him right away."

Grace's face took on a more serious expression. "Honey, there is no reason you should not have a friend to share a part of your life. David is never going to wake up one day and magically return to the way he used to be. Considering all you've told me, I think that you have done all you can. Does Holly know about Gordon yet? What does she say?"

"I didn't see any point in telling her right now. Sometimes she rushes to judgment and I don't want to start a situation for no reason. That's why it was so important for me to tell you first."

The afternoon had flown away, and it was soon time to leave. I realized we had not heard a sound out of Jack, so he must have been totally absorbed in his television show. I carried the coffee cups to the sink and headed home.

I took the impatient dogs out for a walk in the gathering twilight, pulling on a heavier coat. After the winter sun had gone away it turned sharply colder. Normally I found this to be a very depressing time of the year. However, instead of plodding along with my head down, there was a new spring to my step. One of my neighbors was just pulling into his driveway after a day of work, and I gave him a cheerful wave. He gave me a surprised look, but smiled.

I was still fighting with the invisible naysayer perched on my shoulder who was whispering negative thoughts, but I so desperately wanted a little joy to return to my life that I ignored it.

CHAPTER TWENTY

Instead of retreating to my chair and turning on the television with a bowl of ice cream as I often did, I wandered into the bedroom and opened the closet door. In front of me was a sea of beige, brown, navy, and black. Usually I just grabbed a pair of neutral slacks or jeans, coupled with whichever sweater or shirt was handy, and pulled on a comfortable pair of sneakers.

I sank down on the edge of the bed, remembering how much I used to enjoy shopping. I even recalled making sarcastic remarks about old ladies who dressed as if they had given up. I still made regular visits to the beauty shop to have gray streaks expertly covered up in my dark hair, a habit started long ago. However, it was now overdue, and I thought I looked very drab and old.

I peered into the dresser mirror only to see an aging woman looking back. I had always been careful to use daily sunscreen and never left the house without makeup. My mother applied makeup daily, even when she was spending her last days in a nursing home. I admired her for making this effort and had automatically done the same.

Although I had a large collection of costume jewelry, I rarely found a reason to put most of it on. A large box in the back of the closet contained a number of handbags, but I never changed from the sensible one I carried. Little by little, I had taken the course of least resistance in the past few years.

I had once taken great pride in how I dressed, but there did not seem to be anyone around to give me a second glance now. I often wanted to recede into the background and become invisible. David rarely noticed or gave me compliments, even when we were younger.

It is odd how one remembers insignificant moments of life years later. More than a decade ago, David and I were walking through a mall department store. I had just had my hair done and was wearing a new outfit. I felt good and checked out my image on a large mirror as we walked along.

David gave me a sardonic laugh and said, "What are you looking at? You aren't that great." I was humiliated and did not even reply.

I still watched my weight, but mostly for health reasons. When I saw my sagging, naked body in the mirror, I averted my eyes. After all, I told myself, I was old, so what did it matter? I had never felt I measured up in looks to my friends. I could recall staring at one of my high school classmates who was chosen as cheerleader, homecoming queen, and even a member of the student council. It had never seemed fair she gained everything with her looks. Her long, naturally blonde hair swirled around her graceful neck, and I could not remember ever seeing a blemish on her face.

Common sense told me this was just inherited, and she was not at all stuck up. She was actually very sweet and kind. Of course, this was just another reason why she was so popular. I hadn't seen her for years and could not picture her being different even now, but assumed she had aged well. I envisioned her having married a wealthy successful man, living in a perfect expensive house, with perfect children who were just like her.

I had married David with the knowledge that short, ethnic-looking girls were never chosen as homecoming queen. Boys simply did not even look my way. Some of them asked to copy my homework, but I was mainly treated as a pal. When I used to watch them compete for the attention of the tall, striking girls, I came to accept it as a fact of life.

I was far from being a pretty young thing, so I concluded that folks in my age group were drawn to things other than looks. Gordon had asked me to go out for totally different reasons. I then jumped back to reality. This was just a lonely, nice man looking for a pleasant person to share a meal. He would not care how I looked or what I wore. I was back to being chosen as a buddy.

Well, I thought, there is nothing wrong with that. I began to relax my anxious mind when another thing dawned on me. Good grief! What if he is looking for a new sexual partner?!

I assumed it had been a long time for him. He might assume that I was also needy by now. How would I handle that? Not that this would be a totally bad thing, but I could not imagine baring my misshapen old body to anyone.

I lay awake most of that night thinking about this. I wouldn't really feel comfortable speaking to Grace about it, either. I knew several older couples who had lost their first spouses and found someone else in later life. I pictured each of them and wondered how easily it was to jump into bed with someone new in their 70s or even 80s. Most had bodies even worse than mine, so maybe after a certain age, nobody cared.

After a restless night I came to one main decision. During the shopping trip I should definitely buy new underwear.

I sat down, drank a cup of coffee, and nibbled on a piece of rye toast. Normally I would have eaten a much bigger breakfast, but suddenly I was very worried about losing a few pounds. As I remembered though, Gordon was carrying a few extra of his own.

He was such a nice guy that I would never judge him in that way. And he would have to be a very shallow person to worry about my protruding tummy and ugly upper arms. Old ladies almost always get repulsive arms but they never seem to worry about it. I had stopped wearing sleeveless clothing long ago.

I made myself stop having these crazy thoughts and went to pick up Grace. After all, I was just going out to dinner and my imagination had taken it to another level. Grace rented one of those motorized scooters at the mall and was able to totally keep up with me. I told her I didn't have the slightest idea of what to buy.

I had been to the mall to Christmas shop two years ago, but it was not a place where I felt comfortable. Modern malls are geared to teenagers and young adults. I did most of my shopping online now, but this was not an occasion for that. I casually mentioned to Grace about my need for underwear, and she pointed to one of the large department stores.

I took several items to the dressing room to try on, acutely embarrassed. I had once heard that hidden cameras were installed in some dressing rooms in order to catch shoplifters. I finally figured out what the best choices were, and was astounded by the price tags. This was a lot different than buying inexpensive packages of six or more in a big box store.

It took several more hours to round up a couple of suitable outfits. I was able to find things that looked good on me, and they were having their mid-winter clearance, so it was the perfect time to buy. I ended up with a fitted pants outfit in deep hunter green, and despite my protests, Grace insisted I buy a long burgundy skirt with sweater to match.

Our next stop was at one of the shoe stores. Thanks to encouragement from Grace, I walked out a bit later with a pair of knee-high soft black leather boots, some basic flats, and a more youthful pair of sneakers than the ones I usually chose.

On the way out of the mall, Grace spotted a stylish black coat with leather trim. Even if I wasn't having this dinner date, it made me feel very good to have new clothing.

"Oh wait," she said. "Take those packages to the car and come right back in." Assuming she was hungry by now and wanted to head down to the food court, I was happy to comply. We chose corn chowder and small salads, and I did not feel too guilty eating it.

I enjoyed sitting there and hearing Grace comment on how people were dressed and other common mall sights. We watched children ride the big carousel and saw numerous signs advertising upcoming Valentine's Day specials. For many years I had felt a painful stab of jealousy when I knew that countless others would be receiving flowers, candy, or gifts. I had tried to explain to David that it wasn't about something expensive — it was just about being remembered. A sincerely given single rose or even a card would have made me happy. Like so many other occasions, this was ignored. Long ago, I had come to the painful conclusion that gifts and cards mean nothing if they have to be prodded. Mother's Day, anniversaries, and other days of being loved and honored were not much different than any other day for the largest portion of my years.

I shook these thoughts away. Grace was smiling and saying that we weren't quite done. She pointed me to the department store cosmetic counter.

"Now, dear, I am not saying you don't do fairly decent with makeup, but it can't hurt to let an expert help a bit."

Before I knew it I was sitting in a tall vanity chair, letting a simpering young man apply new makeup to my face. I was skeptical at first, but actually liked the results. A collection of very expensive cosmetics were soon in a bag, and I almost passed out while signing the credit card bill.

By now, Grace was worn out, and we left for home. I was ready for my big dinner date.

CHAPTER TWENTY-ONE

I was increasingly nervous as the time approached for Gordon to pick me up. I had sent him my address then spent several hours getting dressed far in advance of the time he had said he would be there. I perched nervously on the couch. By the time the doorbell actually rang, I was almost sick to my stomach.

I had chosen to wear the burgundy skirt outfit with my new boots. I almost took it off and was wondering if I was overdressed and would look silly. There could be nothing more pathetic than an older woman trying to recapture her youth in a bad way.

I had recently observed someone my age who had chosen to dye her hair platinum blonde. It was styled in long curls, and she looked like an over-the-hill hooker. In such heavy contrast to her face, which really looked her age, it was like a Halloween outfit. I actually felt sorry for the lady. She was obviously trying to retain her beauty, but not in a very tasteful way. I would never want to look like this.

I took a deep breath and opened the door. My fears fell away when I saw a smiling Gordon standing there. He was wearing a casual shirt and jacket, topped by a lightweight raincoat.

"Hi Kate," he said.

I thought his voice sounded just a little nervous.

"I am so glad you agreed to go out to dinner. I've been feeling so alone now for such a long time. Even my friends do not really understand. They've been so supportive from the beginning, but this is kind of a long-term bad dream. It takes someone else who has lived it to really feel what every day is like."

I had let him into my little living room, apologized for the dogs, who were always very inquisitive with strangers, and took his coat. I offered a drink, which he declined, and we were now to the foot-shifting awkward part.

"Oh, sorry for rushing into saying all of that," Gordon apologized. "I didn't mean to be so forward. I guess I've just been bottling up so much inside that it was ready to spew out of my silly mouth!"

"No, no," I said, "I totally understand. As you said, after a while, your friends don't even ask anymore. Having one's spouse in a long-term situation is not what someone wants to hear about all the time. I could even sense an air of relief when people didn't have to figure some new words of comfort when I saw them."

"Exactly!" Gordon said. "I have had old and dear friends who had to deal with deaths, and I felt like I was there for them. Gradually their lives returned to some sense of normalcy, and they got on with daily things. This never changes. We are in a kind of limbo. My best friend I used to go fishing with has a typical story. He and his wife were the perfect couple. When she got cancer and died, I thought he was never going to heal. I tried everything I knew to help, but he wallowed in grief for a very long time."

"One summer, my cousin came to town for a visit. This was about a year before Mary Anne's accident. We had a weekend barbecue, and I invited my buddy. Before the evening was over, I could see that he and my recently-divorced cousin had taken a shine to each other."

"She mentioned an old rock star was in town, and they both seemed to be long-time fans, so he asked her to go with him. A relationship quickly blossomed and they were married on Christmas Day."

"Yes," I said, "I have several friends who have found a second chance. However, having a spouse in this situation is so very different. There are no deaths, no divorces, and virtually no hope. We just have to walk through each day doing our duties, never shirking away from seeing to their care, but the person is more or less gone,"

"Okay," Gordon said, as he stood up. "Enough of this. I think we well know how it works. Let's go and eat a good meal and find another subject to talk about."

As we headed out the door, he remarked that his BMW was in the shop so we would have to take the work car. I have heard other people make a similar joke, so I just smiled and said it was fine. Sure enough, the older car that I had ridden in previously was at the curb. He opened the door for me and we were off.

Gordon mentioned a new restaurant had just opened across town and that he had heard positive things. I assured him I was not picky and anything was fine. When we arrived there was a parking attendant. This seemed like a very expensive place.

We were seated right away, and I could tell that it was indeed a very high-class eatery. I had already concluded he probably had to spend a lot of money to keep Mary Anne in the care facility, and I felt a pang of guilt. I hoped he didn't think he had to impress me.

A smiling waiter soon came to take our order. I politely ordered water, refusing the offer of wine. I was appalled by the prices on the menu, and searched for something affordable.

Gordon looked at the choices thoughtfully and said, "Kate, I am really trying to watch what I eat, but you order anything you want." He laughingly patted his tummy, as if to illustrate the extra pounds he was trying to lose.

He pointed to an entrée of broiled codfish with a side salad when the waiter came back with his order book. I took this as a hint and said I would have the same.

We spoke a little about how hard it was to keep away from the things we used to eat all the time, like French fries and ice cream. I hoped Gordon would never open my freezer and see the ice cream I still could not resist.

We went on to telling each other about our lives, and I tried to keep from telling the long stories. Gordon told me his father had practically forced him to go to medical school, while he had desired to pursue music.

"I wanted to maybe teach music to youngsters, perhaps as a high school teacher, or even in college. But my father saw me as a doctor, smitten with all the advantages that came with it. In the end, I did it his way and discovered it to be very rewarding. Of course, I made a good salary, and we were able to give our son all he needed or wanted."

"I actually met Mary Anne in college, and we hit it off right away."

I couldn't help but notice the sadness in his eyes while remembering this. I felt a wave of guilt that I was out on a kind of fake date with a man who loved another woman so much. She wasn't, after all, dead. My situation with David was a little the same, but very different.

I had only spoken the most basic facts about my earlier years, and especially left out most of the facts about David.

It was satisfying to finally have someone listen to me with interest and patience. Of course, Grace had hung on every word as I told her the really long version of my life. I was not quite ready to tell this to Gordon.

When we arrived back at my home, Gordon saw me to the door, gave me a little kiss on the cheek, and remarked on how nice the evening had been. As I said all the right words to thank him, I found myself inviting him to come over for a home-cooked meal the following week. I could tell by the look on his face that this idea pleased him.

Goodness gracious, what was I getting myself into?

CHAPTER TWENTY-TWO

I wasn't surprised when my phone rang early the following morning. I knew I would be hearing Grace's voice.

"Oh, honey, I hope I am not calling too early! I just had to know what happened. Tell me everything!"

I quickly related the events of my "date," and added it was just dinner with a friend. I went on to tell her I was worried about what my children would say if they knew I was "keeping company" with another man. Even though both of them realize how hard it had been for me since David had become so much worse, I did not think they would approve.

My daughter had a tendency to be judgmental about a lot of things, right down to my decisions on spending money, daily activities, and even my hairstyle. I realized a long time ago that she meant well, just trying to keep her mother on the right track, but sometimes I felt smothered. Holly lives in Florida and I totally understood that she had to live her own life. She calls or emails every few days, but it is mainly just checking in, without time for long conversations.

Eric had his own set of responsibilities, even though he lives nearby. If I called him and asked for help in something, he would work it into his time and not complain. However, I rarely felt right about doing this. I never spoke of my daily feeling of being trapped in this situation to either of them.

Without having to think about it all that much, I had decided it was much better to keep most things to myself. I knew it was a relief to both my children when I assured them there was really no reason to visit their father. I did not want them to feel guilty about this.

But I knew they would have an opinion about any major changes I might make without consulting them. I could barely explain or justify spending time with Gordon to myself, let alone finding the right words to tell my children.

I briefly told this to Grace to see if she agreed. This remarkable old lady had come to be my best friend and main confidant. I marveled at the seemingly accidental meeting that led me to her and Jack. This reasoning left me to think that running into Gordon had not been random, either. I simply had to believe that things like this were all preordained, and I should just accept it all.

Grace assured me there was no real reason to call up my children and look to find some type of permission to have Gordon in my life.

"As much as I love my kids," she said, "they live their own lives. We keep in touch, but I don't tell them everything I do."

She chuckled under her breath a little after saying this, and it seemed a little curious, but I didn't think all that much about it. After all, how much trouble could this frail woman get herself into?

I realized I actually knew very little about her life, and I suppose I had just assumed it was pretty normal. Obviously, Jack let her do pretty much whatever she wanted, and I never had the slightest hint of any disagreements between them.

At this point I asked if she wanted me to pick her up and go out for a little brunch. I knew she would eagerly agree. She was waiting impatiently when I arrived, with Jack seemingly enjoying the newspaper. She gave him a peck on the cheek, and

I helped her to the car. I noticed she could get around much better than she seemed able to all those weeks ago when we first met. She still relied on her walker sometimes, but when she didn't have to walk too far, a cane was all that was necessary.

We went to one of our favorite local restaurants and ordered croissants, fruit, and coffee. I told her more details about my evening, including the fact that I was planning to cook him a meal. We discussed what this meal could be, and so on. Grace often wore this little smile when something pleased her. The expression in her eyes never seemed to be what one would expect to see in an older person. Soon, an hour had passed.

"Jack will be wondering about me," she said, and that was the signal to leave.

I made a mental note to ask her about her past. We were usually discussing my life and she had seemed more than happy to keep it that way. I would also like to see photos from her youth. I pictured a very beautiful young person. I had noticed she did not have lots of framed photos displayed around her little apartment as most older folk do.

We made arrangements to have a light supper later on at her home. I offered to bring something but Grace assured me she could order simple things from her favorite deli and that they would deliver it. I paced like a caged tiger for most of the day. Just two very innocent outings with a man that I barely knew had made me feel so very differently about life. Later on, while nibbling on an amazing chicken salad sandwich made with toasted wheat bread, I expressed my conflicted feelings to Grace.

She was wearing a lovely floral print long robe, and, as usual, looking flawless. The bright lettuce green of the print was perfect for her complexion. I could hear the television playing in the bedroom and assumed that Jack had already retired for the day. After hearing me pour my heart out to her about letting myself have too many expectations about Gordon, she shook her head back and forth like a little bird.

"Kate," she scolded me, "have you always overthought every single thing in your life?"

I had never heard her speak this forcefully to me before, and my mouth dropped open in surprise.

"My sister Janice almost threw away a lifetime of happiness because she could not force herself to stop trying to please everyone. She married in haste just out of school. I was only sixteen then, but it was plain to me she had made a big mistake. After only a few months, she began to tell me how sad she was."

"I told her to leave this guy and come home. However, this was back in the days when girls were supposed to marry forever, so she did not think it possible. Her husband was older, a widower, and just needed a wife. Janice never thought she was very pretty, so she jumped at the chance to marry. Day by day, her eyes became dull and lifeless, and it broke my heart."

"They lived on a little farm and the daily chores were hard in those days. She soon stopped smiling and began to look like a much older person. During the next harvest season her husband hired a young man to help out, and he and Janice soon became friends. She was very careful to keep this from her husband, but she did confide in me. I begged Janice to leave her husband and seek happiness with this new friend. She told me he was planning on heading south in the autumn, seeking a new opportunity for his life."

I was almost afraid to ask, but Grace had me feeling so sorry for this young woman I hadn't even known about a few minutes earlier.

"I have to know. Did your sister have a terrible life?"

"Actually," she said, "things have a way of working out. Her husband had a terrible accident just a few weeks later. He was alone in the barn and must have taken a misstep. He fell out of the hayloft and broke his neck."

"Janice was away helping sew a quilt at her church that afternoon, so nobody could think she had anything to do with the accident. Even the young man, whose name was Tom, was across the county working for another farmer that day."

"Her husband had no other family, so Janice inherited the farm and everything. After a decent time had passed, she married Tom and they had a wonderful life together. She gave birth to five children, all boys. Both she and Tom are gone now, but they had many happy years."

I felt a pang of relief and wondered how I could be so happy for a girl that I had never met.

This story gave me a good opening, so I asked Grace about her earlier life. I had inquired before but not learned very much. I told her how unfair it was for me to burden her with so many of my problems when I knew so little about her. I mentioned I was curious about the lack of photographs. I so wanted to see what she looked like as a young child.

"Oh, my dear, I really don't like to think back all that much. As for photos, we lost all my baby pictures in the fire."

CHAPTER TWENTY-THREE

I turned to her with wide eyes and said, "Fire??"

Grace sighed, then slowly spoke, "I prefer not to think about those days, honey, and really saw no point in bringing it up. I've sensed you have been wanting to ask me questions. I really thought that I needed to listen to you. I read people pretty well, and from the day we met I could see how badly you needed someone to talk to."

"Well, Grace, that is true, but I did not mean to show a total lack of interest in your life. I guess I assumed you and Jack have had a fairly smooth past, one much more normal than mine. What fire?"

"Kate, if I remember correctly, one of the first things you told me was that you had to go back to the beginning or I would not understand your present day. I suppose that is true of my life, too. Seeing Jack and I now most assuredly does not give you any insight of the past."

"I am very old," the lady said with a little laugh, "so you might assume that things had to be pretty good for me to survive this long. Granted, I have been to the funerals of a lot of people. I am very thankful to have made it this far, but it hasn't been all roses and rainbows!"

"My early years were so long ago that it almost seems to

have happened to someone else. I haven't always lived in Indiana, you know. I moved here after I married Jack. I grew up in Chicago, in a big run-down house on the South side. Something struck a chord in me when you spoke of your longing for a father. I never knew mine, either. I am not at all sure that mother even knew who he was."

"We took in roomers just to get by. Many didn't stay long. Men looking for work came to Chicago just hoping to land a job. They came and went. My brother and I learned to go out on the street and find ways to make a little money when we were quite young. My sister that I mentioned to you earlier stayed around home and helped our mother with the household chores."

"I used to have some singing talent, so my brother played on an old guitar left behind by one of those guys who stayed with us. We went down by the train station and stood on the platform, performing a few short songs. We didn't make much, but some people threw change in the guitar case we put out. The policeman on duty there was a nice man. He felt sorry for two small children, I guess. I didn't realize it until later on, but he kept an eye out for our safety. I saw him chase off other panhandlers."

"There was an Italian restaurant in our very ethnic community. Immigrants from many places lived in the area. I heard languages spoken that I did not understand. The man who owned the restaurant saved leftovers for us, and we often stopped by on our way home from performing. Robert, my brother, and I greedily ate a lot of it, but we took as much as we could home to mother and my sister."

"I was only about ten or so, but I felt very proud to be helping out. My mother never seemed happy. I guess she was just resigned to a life of hard work. Sometimes she slapped us when she was tired or worried. Looking back now, I know she lulled herself to sleep with a bottle of cheap whiskey. We mostly raised ourselves. I never knew any other members of her family. She had a disagreement with her father as a teenager and left home. After being on the streets for a few years she got a factory job. Our building was set to be torn down, but somehow she got permission from the city to live in it."

"In that area of Chicago, most laws were not enforced. People were left alone if they didn't cause trouble. Ma never actually married. We all had different fathers. She loved to tell fabulous made-up stories, and told us we came from royalty and celebrities."

I tried to picture this tiny old lady as a young girl. I saw her as one of those spunky children we sometimes read about or see in movies. However, as she spoke, I began to see something change in her eyes. Memories of hard times will do that to folks, I thought.

"The truant officer came to our house frequently. We attended the ancient brick grade school part of the time, but mostly, we roamed the streets. The sharp-featured lady who came by to threaten my mother would say she would roast in hell for not taking proper care of us. She drove a rusty old Ford, and we were afraid she would throw us into it and we would never be seen again. But that never happened. There just wasn't any funding in those days to remove children."

"It wasn't a bad life until one particular night. A new man had taken one of the upstairs rooms. I was scared of him from the day he arrived. He looked dirty, with an untrimmed black beard and harsh look on his face. I already knew what alcohol smelled like, and he reeked of it. It wasn't long before he found reasons to touch me and my sister. He seemed to especially favor me."

"But he had a pocket full of cash, so my mother turned a blind eye. We hadn't had many people staying there that December. Many vagrants went South during the hard Chicago winters. When this man came along we were even more desperate for money than ever. There were no other renters with us.

Christmas was coming and we children figured Santa would not find us. My mother told us that even old St. Nick was hard up that year. He probably wouldn't have enough toys for all children."

"Robert and I found a scraggy, discarded tree and brought it home. Some of the branches were broken and it was really ugly, but we draped it in popcorn and bits of yarn. Mother said we could stick the stubs of a few old candles on the branches, but only light it for a few minutes on Christmas Eve."

"To us, it seemed like the most beautiful thing. On December twenty third, we children went to bed early because we'd been invited to Christmas Eve church services by a kindly neighbor lady. I hadn't been asleep long when I felt someone slip into my bed. I could tell just by the odor who it was and I opened my mouth to scream. A dirty hand was put over my mouth, while the other hand lifted up my gown. He groped between my legs while slurring drunken words."

"I had a big stick under my bed that we used as a makeshift baseball bat. I reached under there and frantically felt for it. I finally got it into my hand and hit him in the face. He reeled back and fell. I hit him again and again until I knew he was dead. I sat back on the floor, breathing hard and in what I suppose was shock."

By now, I had started making little noises and had my hand up to my mouth. When I agreed to listen to Grace's story, I never dreamed about hearing anything like this. This sweet person had killed a man! I tried to picture her at age 10. I just sat and shook my head, unable to say a word.

Grace stopped speaking and gave me a very serious look.

"I suppose you know you cannot ever repeat any of this. Of course, it was all a long time ago, and I could just say I made it all up."

I shook my head rapidly from side to side, saying, "No, of course I won't tell anyone. But what happened then?"

"Well, honey, here comes the best part. I pictured being arrested and taken to jail. I knew no one would believe a little girl. I sat there and tried to get myself together. I pulled my blood-soaked gown over my head and put on some other clothing. I went to the dresser and retrieved a sock filled with what little cash I had saved. I put on several sweaters and stepped into my worn boots."

"I had learned to put on the face I needed to get by with stuff. I awakened my brother and sister and told them I heard they were giving away food down at the station and we had to go right away. At the last minute I went into my mother's room and told her the same story. She became angry and slapped me hard for waking her up. As always, she had turned to drink when life got too unbearable. Being a mother just wasn't easy for her — we represented past mistakes. I stood there for a moment, then made the hardest decision I ever had to."

Grace stopped and gave me a look. "Kate, you have to understand, sometimes there is no good answer to problems in life."

She went on to say she had told her brother and sister they would have to go quickly. She made sure they were dressed warmly and took them out on the porch. After a minute, she told them it would be so pretty if they could come home and see the Christmas tree all lit up.

"I ran back in, grabbed the box of matches off the mantle, and lit all of the little candle stubs sitting on the already dry pine branches. I looked into the house for just a second, then shut the door behind me. There was no turning back."

"The three of us ran down the snowy sidewalk to the station. The waiting room was almost entirely empty, with only an elderly man asleep on one of the benches. Funny the things you remember. The guy had soiled himself and you could smell him all over that room. In later years, that odor always took me back to this night."

"Robert looked so disappointed and asked where the food was. I told him maybe we were too early and that we should wait. I made them sit on the other bench. I can remember my heart beating so hard I thought they'd be able to hear it."

"After a while, my sister started to complain, "Grace, there is no food, and I am tired. Let's go home to bed." I told her we would wait five more minutes. Just after that, I heard a fire truck screaming down the street."

"As we left the station I saw a big orange glow a few blocks away. I did not want to alarm the others, so I made myself walk slowly. When we got closer to home, I saw the last of our old roof fall in. I joined my brother and sister in screaming and crying. The fire chief turned to us and said, "Oh my gosh, we were afraid you children were inside, too. That old wooden house went up quickly, and nobody got out.""

CHAPTER TWENTY-FOUR

I was frozen to my chair in total disbelief after hearing Grace tell this story. She carefully watched my face, trying to figure out what my reaction would be. I composed my expression, and did the only thing that I could.

"Grace, I totally understand how that night must be etched into your mind. However, you had already shouldered so much more than any child ever should. I think you did the only thing you could. However, I have to know — what happened to you children? Did your brother and sister ever suspect anything?"

She responded slowly. "Let me begin by saying I have never told all of this to anyone. I told much of it, of course, and even said how much I blamed myself for lighting the candles. I always summoned up tears for that part. Right away, folks comforted me, and assured me that it was just one of those tragic things that happen. Who would blame a little girl for making a hasty bad choice?"

"That same night we were taken in by a nice lady who went to the neighborhood church. She had cared for foster children before. However, we ended up living in what used to be called an orphan's home. It wasn't much, but we had regular meals and donated clothing. We had to go to church and learn all of the Bible stories."

I was still trying to take this all in. Grace had a past I would never have dreamed of. How she ever pulled her life together seemed nearly unbelievable. She was sitting there right now, smiling at me, with a normal expression on her face. There had to be a lot more to this.

While I had been pouring out my personal story to her, assuming that she had experienced an average life, she was holding all of this inside. I almost felt guilty now and started to apologize.

"Oh, Grace, I feel so silly now about telling you all the things from my family and how I've let it make me feel. I want to go back and find the little girl you were and give her a hug!"

Grace was quick to shake her head and pat my arm. "Oh, no, Kate, I didn't tell you this story to upset you. I just wanted to give you some insight into what happened to me. Look, you can see I was able to have a good life. That was all so long ago that it almost seems as if I have lived two different lives. Besides, don't you want to hear what happened next?"

"Of course I do!" I said. "You already told me about your sister, but I understand now why she was so much in a hurry to get married."

"Yes, that is the reason. While we spent the next years living with a few dozen other orphans, we were cared for and never went hungry. We had chores to do and the basic necessities of life, but she missed our mother more than Robert and I did. She was the one who was always at home helping with the housework, cooking, and so on. Robert and I had learned more about the world and figured out how to make the system work for us as much as possible."

"Right away, he and I knew how to be what the adults expected of us. We were polite and always put smiles on our faces. People who run homes like that spend much more time with the troublemakers. Robert never suspected anything about the night of the fire, I am happy to say."

"When we had opportunities, we sneaked into the kitchen and stole small amounts of food and hid it. There is a way to be a good thief. Never take enough to be noticeable. Always be in character. Never allow anyone to see anything else."

I continued to be amazed as I listened to Grace. I began to wonder if she had fooled me in any way. There was a lot to think about.

She continued. "Kate, for several years, things just went on. I tried to comfort my sister because she cried herself to sleep every night. In so many ways, she seemed younger than me. I think the one thing that helped her was when a five-year-old girl was brought to the home. Sometimes it makes everything better when a person can help others. My sister started to take care of that little girl because she was so sad and scared. We later found out her mother had abandoned her at a church. She remembered that her mother's new boyfriend didn't want any children around."

"Her name was Carrie, she said, but didn't know her last name. In those days, there was no way to trace children. It didn't take long for her to accept living at the home. After the waiting period was over, she was adopted by a kind couple who wanted a little girl."

"It was hard to see Carrie leave us, but we were happy for her. When I was older I looked for her, but didn't even have a last name to go on. Other children came and went, but like us, many had to stayfor a long time. Many of them felt like brothers and sisters."

I tried to imagine what it must have been like for Grace and the others. She told of occasional outings and how they each received one small gift at Christmas. She spoke of how little was available for them so much of the time. Being an orphan during the Great Depression was not easy.

"When we became teenagers we knew our time at the home was limited. There was a program to go and live with families, often on farms, and work for our keep. We girls were lucky enough to be placed together, but Robert went someplace else. There was no choice. No one cared that we had no way to stay in touch. I hadn't seen Robert cry for a long time, but he did when they came and took him. It broke my heart to stand and watch him go."

I felt tears welling up as I heard this story. This sounded like what happened to black slaves before the Civil War. They were often separated when they were sold to other plantation owners. It was not at all unusual to never see their families again.

"We girls lived on a modest farm and were treated kindly, but we had hard work to do. We could go to class, but had to rise early and do a lot before the time to head for the one-room school. We shared a small bedroom at the back of the house. It was cold in the winters and very hot in the summer. My sister talked all the time about how she could not wait to be old enough to leave. That is how she ended up in her first sad marriage. I am just happy that most of her later life was good. I felt responsible for it all, you know."

"After she left I stayed on and had a part time job in town. I had to walk to get there. One day, it was raining and I was soaked. I heard an old truck coming and stepped out of the way. I was always somewhat afraid of meeting strangers on that lonely road. After the truck went by, the driver put the brakes on, and turned around."

"A young man rolled down the window and gave me a friendly smile. He told me to hop in. I knew not to accept rides from strangers and kept walking. By now, it was raining harder. My hair was plastered to my head and my shoes were filled with water. He drove slowly alongside me, and gave in to laughing at the sight. I finally made the decision of my life and got in. I was pretty sure I was going to be murdered or worse. He handed me an old towel to wipe off with. He turned to me with that big grin and said, "Hi, my name is Jack."

CHAPTER TWENTY-FIVE

A t this point I started asking questions, but Grace shook her head.

"Honey, telling all of that has totally worn me out. This old story isn't going away. We can continue some other time. I don't like re-living a lot of my earlier life. Some things are better left buried in the past. As you told me, I feel strangely able to tell you things that have never been related to anyone."

"But Grace, you can't leave me hanging now," I stammered out. "I never had a single clue that your past was so colorful. I have to know what happened next."

"Now, did I say that I wasn't ever going to continue?" Grace said, with her sweet smile. "I'm sure we can do this the same way you told me all of your family's past. Besides, there's a lot of your story that is still a mystery to me. So, we are going to have to engage in a lot more sessions."

I gave her a hug and reluctantly left. How silly it had been for me to assume that Grace's life had been just average, almost boring. I had so many things to think about. For a little while I had almost forgotten about Gordon, let alone David. Grace had been so very correct. There was so much I had not told her. I now felt much more at ease about trusting her with the biggest family story.

Before going to bed I sat down and wrote a grocery list of

items I would need to make a nice meal for Gordon. After David was no longer was there to cook for, I had fallen into the habit of just having simple things around. I ate mostly soups, salads, and sandwiches. I got out the green recipe box and looked through it. Right there in the middle was the faded paper I knew so well. It was titled simply French Mushroom Soup. The recipe had been recopied several times, but mine still appeared to be very old. I knew it was time to share one more tale with Grace.

I pulled out instructions for a casserole, fancy pasta salad, and chocolate pie. I had no idea what Gordon even liked, but I had made these items many times and felt confident in them. I added their ingredients to my shopping list as well as a few other things. At the last minute I added "Wine?"

I had not bothered to get out the set of my favorite china for a long time. I had sold so many things, but I was now glad I had kept this. I thought back to the very day I had picked them out. David and I were at a flea market and this set of delicate floral dishes had caught my eye. The set we had used for years was in an old-fashioned pattern and I was ready for something new. As expected, David told me I was buying cheap junk and could not understand why I would replace the "better set." I bought the china I liked that day, and was now happy that I had.

I spent the week cleaning the house. I picked out a nice butter yellow tablecloth and put away the old faded one. It had been a while since I had readied my home for visitors.

When I went to do my grocery shopping, I also dropped in to see David. They had placed him into a wheelchair and pushed him down to the large activity area. He was watching two elderly ladies put an oversized jigsaw puzzle together. I tried, as always, to speak to him in a normal way. I asked how he was and made small talk about the weather and other easy subjects.

I suppose that deep down, on each visit, I wondered if he would respond normally. I looked into his blue-gray eyes to see if I could catch a spark of recognition. This day was no different than any other. He ignored the questions I had asked and told me his wife was cooking lunch. He said she made really good meatloaf and that I could stay and have some. I responded in a way to keep him calm. Of course, I had learned to do this long before he had become ill. He now saw me as a stranger, and that is how I had felt for a long time.

I stopped at the main nurses' station to see if there was anything I needed to know. As I approached, I saw a very familiar face. Gordon was speaking with two of the nurses and they all had very serious looks on their faces.

They handed him a paper to sign, and he hastily scribbled his name.

The older nurse said, "Doctor, they might be transferring her over to the hospital in a couple of hours. I am sure everything will be fine, but pneumonia could be very serious for Mary Anne right now."

Gordon nodded in agreement and I could see that he was very concerned. He looked up, surprised to see me.

"Mary Anne has gotten pneumonia and they could be putting her in the hospital. I only wish she could remember who I am. She seems to get farther away every time I am here. They say that patients with severe head injuries slowly withdraw, but I am always hopeful."

I told him about my visit with David and said I would understand if he could not come for the dinner I had planned. He said that he was still going to come, though.

"I will closely monitor her condition of course, but I gave up sitting for hours at her bedside a long time ago. She only saw me as a nice stranger, anyway. On her best days there was nothing I could figure out to say. I guess I will go and call my son." I gave his arm a little pat before he walked away.

I was happy to hear he was still coming to dinner. I felt guilty thinking this, but I would have felt like a child having to cancel a party.

The two nurses were looking at me curiously. They had not heard our conversation. I hastily said that we had met in the elevator. That was true, after all.

"Well, Mrs. Williams, there is not much to tell about David. He doesn't eat very much any more, but that is just part of his condition." I nodded, and thanked them.

I kept busy all week so I did not have time to visit Grace and Jack. We had a few brief conversations, and I called to tell her about Gordon's wife. I asked her opinion about maybe visiting poor Mary Anne, but Grace immediately told me that this was a bad idea.

"What if one of her friends or family members were there? How could you explain your connection? Besides, it is much better for you to never to see her in person. I know you Kate, and you would feel such guilt that you would never see Gordon again."

I realized she was correct, so I focused on the dinner. When Saturday arrived, I carefully measured out the ingredients and concentrated on making this the best food I had cooked in a long time. That morning I had run out to the neighborhood grocery to buy fresh flowers and crusty Italian rolls.

I decided to dress simply in a pair of jeans with a green plaid shirt. Someone had given me a pretty apron a few years ago, so I decided this would be a nice touch. Before long the doorbell rang, and a smiling Gordon was standing on the porch. The dogs had to bark for a few minutes, but they soon decided he was not an enemy. I was glad to see him welcome them onto his lap on the sofa. I usually judged people by their interaction with my dog babies.

"I just have a few things to do," I said nervously, "and, then we will be ready to eat."

Gordon said all the right things, like complimenting my home and mentioning how good the bubbling casserole in the oven smelled. I bit my lip when I burned my finger taking it to the table. I told myself to settle down.

I was hoping for a very pleasant evening.

CHAPTER TWENTY SIX

As we sat down to eat, I politely asked about Mary Anne. Despite everything, I knew Gordon loved this poor woman, and every day was like a horrible nightmare to him. The person he remembered so dearly was gone forever, and it was difficult to witness the pitiful way she had to spend her days. I thought of the parallel between her and David, who seemed so remarkably alike. Of course, many others who lived in Pine Haven were also in this suspended state. I had run into an old friend whose mother lingered on there for several years. David had only been at the facility for a few weeks when we met in the cafeteria.

I gazed into my friend's tired eyes and could only imagine how hard this had been for her and her family. It was only a month or so later that the tortured lady finally passed away. She was quite old, but I knew that did not take away the acute loss my friend was feeling. I usually avoid funerals, but in this case I decided to go. When I gave my friend a hug and spoke the usual condolences, I saw actual relief on her face.

Gordon told me his wife was being given massive doses of antibiotics and was on oxygen to help her breathing. I could see he felt totally helpless.

"Being a doctor myself doesn't make situations like this any easier," he said. "I have had to give families bad news about their loved ones so many times, but sometimes, there are just no words."

He went on to say he was thankful to come visit and have the company.

"I've had to go home so many times alone, and try to find a way to sleep and eat a little. Mary Anne has had other sicknesses. Several times she appeared to be having a panic attack. They gave her meds to calm her down, but that's a horrible sight."

I could tell that Gordon had enjoyed the meal, and he helped me clear the table. We sat down on the couch and struggled to find a safe subject to talk about. The dogs joined us and we compared notes on all the pets we had once owned and loved. Gordon's eyes misted over when he discussed a German shepherd he and Mary Anne had adopted when they were newly married.

"I was still a resident and putting in really long hospital hours. It made me feel so much better that Lady was in the house with my wife. She was still with us when my son was born, and protected him, too. It was one of the saddest times of my life when Lady got older and had pain in her hips when she walked. We got medicine from the vet, but it was soon time to let her go. We both held her while we said goodbye. I'll never forget the trusting look she gave me just before she went. We went out to the car and cried for a long time. It is memories like this that make the current situation so much harder."

I realized tears were rolling down my cheeks as I listened to this story. David and I had similar situations in the past, but he never seemed to let it all affect him as much as it did me. A beautiful blonde cocker spaniel appeared one day. She was very thin and we knew she had been on her own for a while. I was secretly happy that nobody answered the lost dog ads I placed. I named her Gypsy, and she was my best companion. The children were in grade school then, and that sweet little dog was always by my side. I told her all my problems, crying into her glossy coat more than once.

After she was with us for almost a decade, I found a lump on her thigh. It turned out to be malignant. Despite the vet care we gave her, it was soon apparent her quality of life suffered. I took her on that last ride alone and grieved for days. I could remember wishing David would just hold and comfort me, but he wasn't like that.

We spoke of other animals and found humorous stories about many of them. It felt good to laugh with this man.

Gordon was just saying he should go when his cell phone rang. He glanced at it to see who was calling and hastened to answer the call. I saw his expression change as he listened to the person on the other end. A light left his eyes as if someone had turned off a switch.

He sank back on the couch and stared off into space for a few minutes. I sat there silently, waiting for him to speak.

"She's gone," he finally said. "The nurse said they thought she was actually getting a little better, but when they went back to check on her, she had died."

I quietly said how sorry I was, but he wasn't hearing me. He continued to sit there for a few more minutes, processing it all. He finally jumped up and grabbed his coat.

"I have to go, Kate, there's much to do. I don't know how long I will be tied up, but I will call you when I can."

He patted my shoulder and was out the door. I had a variety of emotions, also, but ended up feeling badly that this news seemed like a relief to me. I was tremendously conflicted about being so drawn to this wonderful man.

I slowly washed the dishes and put them away. I could never have predicted how this evening was to end. I glanced at the clock and decided it was way too late to call Grace. She had turned into the person I first thought of when anything happened in my life. I wryly wondered how I had survived before we had met.

I fed the dogs, let them out on the patio for a few minutes, and checked to be sure everything was locked up. I had done this nightly routine so many times that I did it automatically.

As I drifted off to sleep, I realized that I was feeling happy and somehow, much more peaceful than I had in a long time.

CHAPTER TWENTY-SEVEN

A few days later I read Mary Anne's obituary in the paper. I had not heard from Gordon. This was not surprising. I could imagine all that he was going through. Technically, this man had lost his beloved wife twice. I had no idea if final arrangements were already in place, but there surely were some decisions to be made.

I had called Grace the morning after Mary Anne's death to give her the news, but she said they had a Monday doctor's appointment she had to get ready for, and would have to talk to me later. I was a little shocked she wasn't as eager for details as usual, but perhaps this whole thing was becoming too much for her to deal with. I decided I should not depend on making her into a daily contact. When we met, I had missed having a person to share everything with. I realized this dependency might have become a burden. After all, Grace was an older lady and I did not want to compromise her health.

It was a full week before the funeral, allowing time for Gordon's son to travel back home. Without talking to either him or Grace, I felt very alone. I took the dogs to be groomed, organized my closet, and found other things to do. I noted that neither of these people had even been in my life for a whole year, and yet I had come to gauge my time around them. Of course, much of what I thought about Gordon was probably only in my own mind, anyway. I had only seen him a few times. I chided myself for making too much of all that.

By the time Friday arrived, I realized I hadn't checked in on David, so I steeled myself to make that all too familiar visit. I had started out the door when my phone rang. I was glad to hear Grace's voice.

"Honey, I am so sorry I haven't made time for you this week, especially now. I was silly enough to hurt my ankle last Saturday, and had to visit the emergency room to get it taped up. I didn't want to worry you."

"Oh my, I hope it is better," I quickly said.

"Yes, it healed up fine for an old lady. I always have to be careful how I get around, you know. I was just careless for a minute. I told you a little fib about getting ready for a doctor's appointment last week. I knew you would want to go out of your way to help me in some way."

"Jack has had a cold, so I decided to call a taxi. Our community here has a service to take folks places when necessary, but I didn't want them to fuss over me. The driver was so nice, and even helped me in and out. When people see the elderly, they are usually quick to step up."

"My goodness, Grace," I said, "you should have called me! I have been missing you, anyway."

I often wondered how this frail woman managed to do things. She always looked perfectly groomed and their apartment was spotless. When I asked her about this once, she explained there was a cleaning service included in their fee for the little home.

I offered to drop by for a visit, and she seemed happy about that. I told her I was going to visit with David first. That stop was very predictable, and I didn't stay long. As I looked at my husband, I found it increasingly difficult to think of this man as the same person with whom I had shared everything for all those years. This was just some sad-eyed stranger about whose care I felt totally responsible.

On the way to see Grace and Jack, I stopped and bought a pie. I was trying to limit my sweets, but a piece of hot apple pie seemed like a great comfort today.   Jack's eyes lit up when he saw the dessert. He quickly ate two slices and was predictably fast asleep before long. Grace ate hers in the slow, dainty way I had become accustomed to seeing. We made spicy herbal tea to go with the pie. We were both relishing this treat and did not speak many words until our plates were empty.

I told her briefly about all that I knew regarding Mary Anne's death. Grace sat and thoughtfully nodded while I spoke.

"Kate, I hope you are not feeling any guilt about this. It was a blessing, you know. Nobody would want to linger in that state for months and months. Gordon will grieve, and sooner or later he'll want to see you again."

I actually had been thinking this was an acceptable finish to Gordon's marriage. He was such a nice guy, and living in limbo was just not right. Grace had me pegged — those thoughts filled me with guilt.

"I know that is all true, but I feel terrible that Mary Anne's death clears the way for Gordon to move on."

"My friend," Grace replied, "sometimes you just have to believe that things happen the way they are supposed to. It was at such a good time, too. You and Gordon had been at your house for hours."

I frowned at those words, and asked what she meant.

"Well, it would be terrible if anyone thought he had something to do with her death. You never know these days."

"She was really sick, Grace," I said. "Why would anyone suspect something else?"

Grace thought for a moment before she replied, "I just remember what was said when my first husband passed away."

I did not think there was anything else that would shock me

about Grace's past, but I was greatly surprised at this statement.

"What?" I almost shouted. "You were just telling me about meeting Jack. Didn't you two fall in love and live happily ever after? You had another husband?!"

"I did meet Jack that day on the road, but a lot of things happened before we got married. He took me home, and after that, he knew where I lived. He stopped by a few times, and I guess you could say he flirted with me. I liked him but was still very young."

"Jack accepted a job working in the Texas oil fields later that year, but he promised to write. I waited, but no letters came. After time passed I had to tell myself that he was out of my life. By this point I was quite resigned to being disappointed."

"A couple of years went by and I knew I needed to get on with my life. Back then, girls were expected to either marry or find a way to support themselves, especially in my situation. If I had been in a normal home, with a mother and father, I might have made other choices."

"One day I stopped by the local library. The librarian was a kind woman and we were friends. She frequently talked about her brother, trying to get me to go out with him. Initially, I had no interest at all. He was a plain, serious young man and owned the local florist shop."

"I finally agreed to go to the movies with Isaac. It was an awkward evening. He didn't seem to have any more interest in me than I did him. We made small talk but I had no plans to see him again. However, his sister was persistent and kept pushing us together. None of it seemed right, but one day, she cornered both of us and pointed out how perfect it was that we had found each other. I'm sure she meant well, but soon she was pushing us into marriage. He did have a successful shop and was financially secure, so I agreed to marry him. We had a simple ceremony at the church and I became Mrs. Isaac Ingram before I really knew him at all."

"I was very nervous about the wedding night. I didn't think it would be the romantic experience every young girl dreams about."

"It did prove to be a clumsy event, so I figured he had never done this before. I was both surprised and relieved when he did not seem interested in making love on a regular basis."

"In those days, this side of marriage was never discussed, so I just concentrated on keeping his house and cooking meals. I tried to be thankful for the security I now had. I still thought about Jack, even though it seemed like he had only been passing through my life."

"One day Isaac was tending to some of his flowers at the shop. A bee flew out of one of the big roses and Isaac ran in panic. He told me he was very allergic to bee stings and had to be careful. He laughed when he said this was a bad profession for him."

"As months passed, I had decided to just adjust to this life, but we were nothing like a close loving couple. It was like living with a brother. I thought things would change sooner or later, but eventually he treated me more like a hired housekeeper. We had nothing in common."

As I listened to this story, I became sad for Grace once again.

CHAPTER TWENTY-EIGHT

Hearing this story from Grace was totally unexpected. I had been so wrapped up in my own life that this had totally come out of the blue. After hearing about how she had met Jack, I had, once again, assumed that everything in her life had just sailed smoothly along for years. I sensed she was at a place in telling this story that she wanted to stop. After the months of either telling her about my life or listening to her recount her own earlier times, I could always tell when she was done. I was dying of curiosity about how she finally came to marry Jack, and what had happened to Isaac, but knew it would have to wait.

I cleared away the pie dishes and asked Grace if there was anything else I could do to help her before I left. Her dainty ankle was wrapped in tape, propped up on a cross-stitch-topped footstool.

On the drive home my cell phone rang. It was Gordon. He spoke quietly, and I surmised someone else was close by.

"Kate, as you might guess, I have a lot going on with the funeral, wake, and family here from out of town. I'll be tied up for a while and wanted to let you know."

I assured him I knew how these things worked, and thanked him for calling.

By now, I had developed a love of his soft voice, and wished I knew how long it would be before I heard it again. I felt strangely alone when I arrived home. It was always nice to see how happy the dogs were to see me. They jumped onto my lap as soon as I sank down into my chair. I had bought it after I moved. It was covered in rose patterned chintz and was just my size. David would have hated it.

This thought took me back to the first furniture we had owned as newlyweds. It was sturdy and in the style of that decade, upholstered in an ugly brown and orange tweed. I had hated it on the spot, but David said that was "practical." The matching chair and couch remained in our living room for a long time, until Eric was wrestling around with one of his buddies and they broke off one of the legs. He thought he was in trouble, but I quickly gave him a hug that left him confused.

I hadn't thought about that hideous furniture for a long time. I was transported back to all the years we opened Christmas gifts sitting on that couch. It was very visible in so many holiday photos. Sick children lay on it, threw up on it, and had arguments on it. Once, Eric was jumping on it and had thrown one of Holly's dolls at her in a childish fit of temper. It had hit her just right to chip her front tooth, which cost several hundred dollars to fix. I gave an audible little snort when I remembered that David had blamed me.

"Kate, if you had been watching them this never would have happened. What kind of mother are you?"

In the early years I had taken the bait and replied to comments like this. Nothing was ever resolved when I did, though. I could never figure out how he just blew it all off. There was never an attempt to apologize for any of the hurtful things that casually spewed from his mouth. I finally hardened my heart to all of the insults, jibes, and accusations, and it just went in one ear and out the other.

In spite of it all, I loved David. It was the "bad boy" attraction that drew in so many girls. Plus, he was a dutiful father, making sure we had a nice home, manicured lawn, and could repair almost anything. The small part of his personality that seemed to feed on the verbal barbs he hurled at me was something I could endure and ignore. I had justified it all and accepted it as the cost of my lifestyle. Ironically, he was greatly respected by his peers and I was always amazed at how quickly he was able to switch demeanors.

When I needed to phone him for some reason and a colleague answered the phone, I could frequently hear his voice laughing and talking to someone in the background. When he picked up the phone, a very different voice snarled, "What do you want, Kate?"

As I sat there in my beautiful chair, I mused about how Gordon had lost the companionship of a loving wife, and the sudden loss he must have felt. I felt sure they had their share of arguments like most couples, but I could not picture this soft-spoken man even raising his voice.

I knew he had greatly cut back on seeing patients at the hospital since the holidays, and was planning to retire soon. He had told me he was only continuing to cover shifts for other doctors who wanted family time. He had added it was good for him to have those duties.

Having had to spend various days visiting at hospitals and care homes, I could not help but notice how many senior citizens currently had jobs there. I am sure many of them needed the extra income, but it now became apparent that a job was much better than sitting home alone. I once spoke to a cashier at the cafeteria. She was obviously happy to be there and gave smiling service to everyone in the line of hungry people.

After I took my tray back, I had stopped and engaged her in conversation. I complimented her on such dedication to customer service, and she explained how she had made a whole new group of friends there. After her husband passed, she was home alone for over a year. She could not say enough great things about re-joining the workforce.

I considered how many others there seemed to be, working both there and in other places. Granted, Gordon was a respected doctor, but I concluded he would have continued in any job.

I had worked in a department store office for a while, but in that terrible time when I slowly realized something was happening to David, I had to quit. It was a full-time job just being sure he was having a good and safe day. It did not take long for me to lose track of the friends I had made during the short time I had held my job.

After David had first gone to Pine Haven I tried to visit almost every day, but it did not take long for me to realize I could not mentally nor physically continue to do so. I now went about twice a week. Before that fateful day when I met Jack and Grace, I had spent many other days not even getting dressed. I watched television or tried to read, but I spent way too much time inside my head. My lifelong friends from the old neighborhood avoided me after I moved. I called a few times, but everyone always seemed to be busy.

This was far from how I had envisioned my retirement years. There were a few years when David and I had gone on trips, but it didn't feel quite right. I had seen other couples laughing and talking together in a way we never could.

I was convinced Gordon and Mary Anne had been one of those couples I had envied so many times. Fate had taken her away from him. They would never stand on a beach holding hands and watching the sunset ever again. He must be thinking something very much like that, and I felt so sorry for him. I wondered which was worse — losing something so wonderful, or having never had it to lose. Tears were rolling down my cheeks.

CHAPTER TWENTY-NINE

The next time I saw Grace was totally unexpected. One morning my phone rang very early, waking me up. The dogs, who always slept next to me, had not stirred, and they served as my usual alarm clock. They gave me a look of surprise and annoyance. When I sat up with the phone they were forced to move from their cozy nooks, and I knew it was time to let them out.

I answered with a cautious "hello" as I threw on my robe and slippers, heading to the patio door. It wasn't at all like Grace to call so early, so I was fearful something was wrong. As soon as I let the dogs out I sank down in a chair to listen. She spoke swiftly as I focused my attention.

"Oh, honey, I am sorry to bother you so early, but my very best friend has passed. Her daughter just called me. She was a bit younger than me, but we were close at one time. I can't believe she is gone. A heart attack, they think. I really need to go there. Can you take me? Jack just can't drive to Chicago."

My head was swimming with way too many thoughts for the first five minutes of my morning. For a split second after the phone rang I had hoped it was Gordon. A couple of weeks had passed now, and even though I totally understood what he was probably doing, I was disappointed.

"Chicago?" I said. "That is at least an overnight trip, Grace."

"Oh, no problems there. My friend Margie married well. Her husband was a podiatrist. She lives in a five-bedroom house in Naperville. We don't even have to go into the city, and we can stay in her house. Her daughter said it would be fine."

She hurried on to say we were lucky since the Midwest was having an abnormally warm year and there was no worry about a late winter snowstorm.

I was silent, slowly processing all of this. I would have to call my neighbor to look in on the dogs, cancel my dentist appointment, and figure out a lot of other things.

"Well, Grace, I suppose there's no reason why I can't take you. I can certainly understand your wanting to go if she was a close friend. But we need to form a plan. I assume you are wanting to leave today?"

"Oh, yes, we must. The showing is tomorrow, with the funeral the next day."

I surmised this was a three or four-day trip. A small part of me looked forward to having a good reason for getting away.

I assured Grace we could leave by late morning, then made a few phone calls. Pine Haven had to know my whereabouts, and a call to both the dentist office and my neighbor were quickly completed. I left a voice mail for Eric and sat down to make a list.

I didn't travel much anymore, but had learned long ago that one has to take nearly as much for a few days as for two weeks. I started to grab my little overnight bag but switched to the next size larger. A quick image of how I used to pack for family trips when the children were young flashed through my mind. I had to pack for everyone, of course. It was painful when these memories came up. Before I could totally banish them to the back of my mind, I remembered a young, strong David sitting there beside me, driving us to a vacation.

It had been my job to read the map, and an argument always ensued when I made a mistake. However, I still yearned for those years and was glad I could never have predicted what was coming.

Forcing myself to concentrate on the present, I packed clothing I thought I would need for unpredictable weather. Guessing that Chicago folks would still dress up for funerals, I took my good black dress and the new boots. I remembered how strange it had seemed when casual dress had become the norm in our area for almost every occasion. I was shocked the first time I had seen a man wearing a bright green cap advertising farm machinery to a wedding.

I kissed Mollie and Daisy goodbye and made a quick trip to my neighbor's house, leaving her instructions and the key. I had asked Grace for the address and entered it into my GPS. Assuming we would make a couple of stops, it would certainly be evening before we reached our destination.

I picked up a perfectly groomed Grace, who was wearing a spotless white pants outfit with a pink and lavender scarf around her neck. I helped load her bag then watched her tenderly kiss Jack goodbye. She had arranged for him to get meals delivered while we were gone. She said there was an on-site nurse who could give his insulin shot. I tucked her walker into the back of the car, even though I had noticed she wasn't using it nearly as much lately.

We made small talk as I headed to the interstate, and I asked her to tell me about Margie.

"Oh, she was from a Norwegian family. Many folks from there settled in the Chicago area a century ago. She sure did look the part, with blonde hair and blue eyes. For years, she kept her hair in a long thick braid wound around her head."

"I met her at the grocery store one afternoon. I inquired about all of the vegetables she was buying. We began to talk about cooking and ended up getting coffee later."

"Margie was still living at home then and was dating several young fellows. I was old enough to be her mother, but we hit it off. She told me about her family and I got the impression her real mother was not all that interested in Margie's love life. It was a large family, and being a Norwegian housewife was always filled with duties."

"We only lived a few blocks apart, so she started coming by to visit. We became good friends and she confided in me. She was seeing mainly two different boys. One was a looker and worked in the stockyards. The other was more average looking and in medical school. Handsome Jimmie couldn't afford real dates, so they mainly met in the park or went down to the lakefront just to walk. She packed a little lunch for them."

"Harvey was going to be a doctor. He came from one of the better families, and could take her to nice restaurants and plays. His rather plain looks had kept him from doing a lot of dating. He spoke with a slight stutter and wore horn-rimmed glasses. Margie considered him a really good friend, though, and felt she could tell him anything."

"By the time we met, she was to the place she knew she had to choose one young man. I knew she was leaning toward Jimmie, but was quick to point out how much more secure her life would be if she went the other way.

In the end, she did marry Harvey, and tried to forget Jimmie. I went to her wedding and could see how much her husband loved her. I was sure I had given her good advice. He became a successful podiatrist and they built a nice home. I was there at each birth of her four blonde daughters, and all seemed to be perfect."

"She decorated that big house for Christmas and held events for Harvey's colleagues. Lavish parties were thrown for the girls' birthdays. Margie belonged to all the right organizations and never had to work a day in her life. Harvey doted on her. It seemed to be every little girl's dream."

"One day she was shopping and felt someone tap her on

the shoulder. She turned around to see Jimmie standing there with a big grin on his face. All of the old feelings came rushing back in an instant. They stepped into a café for coffee and conversation. Jimmie had never married and was now a foreman at the stockyards. He had dated other girls but none of them ever seemed right."

"As they continued to laugh and talk, Margie didn't see one of her husband's office girls peer into the window. It didn't take long for the news of this innocent meeting to get back to Harvey. After hearing the man's description, Harvey knew whom Margie was with. He had always been afraid his beautiful wife had never forgotten her other beau."

"I knew Harvey well and could not picture him being a man of anger, but jealousy is a powerful force. He didn't want to have an argument in front of his precious daughters, so he asked Margie to meet him downtown for lunch the next day. She noticed he wasn't acting like himself that day, but didn't think much of it."

"They met in one of those big parking garages. He immediately accused her of having a secret affair with Jimmie, so she told him about the accidental meeting, and swore it was only that one time. By now, Harvey had worked himself into a rage. This was a side of him that Margie had never seen. He grabbed her by the shoulders, told her he would not stand for her being unfaithful, and began to shake the love of his life. She had never dreamed that an innocent cup of coffee would result in this. In his youth, Harvey had been rejected by so many other girls that he totally lost it now."

"In shock, she pushed him away. He slipped on a puddle of oil and tumbled into the path of a large truck. As Margie watched in horror, Harvey died instantly."

CHAPTER THIRTY

I could not believe I was hearing still one more story from Grace that left me astounded. I had assumed her friend had led one of those lives that contained no big drama. I hardly knew what to ask.

"Grace, that is terrible! I have to wonder, did she end up with Jimmie, then?"

"Oh, no, even though she had really done nothing wrong. Her husband's death was kind of his own fault. He didn't give Margie a chance to explain. She was completely faithful to him, even though she had never forgotten Jimmie. After she laid her husband to rest she could not just move on. She never wanted to talk about it, not even to me. She inherited a large amount of money, the house, and some other investments she didn't know about."

"For the rest of her life she concentrated on her daughters and devoted a lot of time to charitable things. If Jimmie ever contacted her, she did not tell me about it. I did think she started to age quickly, though. Now that we know she had a bad heart, perhaps that was to blame. I guess it is possible to literally die of a broken heart, or for one's actual heart to be compromised by a devastating event. The ironic thing is that she had come to really love her homely podiatrist. She was obviously innocent of wrongdoing, but I think she always blamed herself for Harvey's death."

After stopping for lunch we finally arrived in Naperville, and my GPS led us to the house that had been built with such love. The mourning daughters greeted us warmly, and we were shown to our rooms. Only the youngest, Malinda, still lived at home. We could see their eyes were puffy and red-rimmed. Grace was put into a small room on the ground floor to keep her from having to deal with stairs.

Neighbors and friends had carried in a wide array of casseroles, pies, and salads. Large groups of people gathered in the house and it was awkward for me to try to make small talk. They were all strangers, for both me and Grace. An enormous crowd attended the funeral. I was exhausted by the time we left for the drive home. Malinda and her sisters gave us tearful hugs and I had never seen Grace so stressed. I gathered that she had really loved Margie.

We drove in silence for a little while. The first words out of Grace's mouth were, "They are selling the house, you know. They all grew up there, and now they will never be able to return. No holidays, no birthdays, nothing at all. I thought Margie would live to see great-grandchildren. It is so unfair."

I sensed she was much more upset about this than I would have expected. Grace always seemed so levelheaded and calm, even when she had been telling me about her early years. I wanted to ask her a lot more about that, but this did not seem like a good time.

I decided this might be a good opportunity to confide in her about the family mushroom soup recipe. I had wrestled with this for several months. I rarely trusted others, especially with a centuries-old secret. However, considering what she had told me, it seemed obvious that she would understand.

"Grace, I have been wanting to tell you more about my family's past. I have never told this to anyone else, and I think you will be interested. I totally trust you."

Her mood brightened. I paused a moment before speaking.

"Do you remember one of the first stories I told you, concerning my great, great grandmother having to handle a small band of Yankees at the end of the Civil War?"

I could she her struggling to recall the story, so I briefly retold her what had happened.

"At the very end of the war it was not unusual for Yankee soldiers to go off on their own to profit for themselves. They usually looked for small plantations in rural areas. They took anything they wanted, and sometimes even raped the women. The men from those families were most likely still away fighting for the last shreds of the Confederacy."

"This happened at my family's place in Dresden, Tennessee. Belle, my great-grandmother, was still a child, and she was told to go to bed early. She watched her mother bravely greeting the soldiers, almost being friendly. She said she'd use what few vegetables they had left to make them a 'special soup' they would never forget."

"She treated them with Southern hospitality, smiling as she cooked. Before long, a steaming bowl of soup was set before each man. The three of them had ridden down the lane a few hours before, expecting to be met with the same sullen resistance they'd seen before by proud women dressed in faded dresses. A chance to have a hot meal seemed great, so they looked forward to the soup."

"They all ate as much as they could before it was time to sleep for the night. They had put up a little tent in the yard. Lucy also supplied them with a bottle of elderberry wine, and it wasn't long before they were snoring loudly. But in a few hours they began to have extreme gastric pain and lost consciousness again — only they were not to wake up again."

"When our family had first arrived from France to settle in New England, a much earlier grandmother named Cornelia had become friendly with a Native American in a peaceful tribe. He taught her many things about gathering bark, berries, and mushrooms. She learned natural remedies to cure sickness. She also learned how to recognize an extremely poisonous mushroom variety later referred to as the Death Cap. This wise man told her to cautiously gather and dry this mushroom, and keep it carefully stored away. It would rid their cabin of mice and other vermin."

"The family barely got by in those years. The man of the house worked down on the docks unloading ships, and his wife did mending and sold eggs. There was a horrible greedy man who owned the general store and offered them credit. He had done this with others, hoping to take over their land."

"When the bill came due he made a visit to collect, knowing they could not pay. He gave them a paper stating that the constable would be back in a week to lock them out. When their pet dog growled at him, he shot the poor thing. Their young son loved this dog and was heartbroken."

"Now, remember this story has been re-told for generations, but the way it was explained to me is that Cornelia took the very last of her flour, mixed it with some honey and nutmeats, as well as berries. It made delicious cookies. She also added a generous scoop of those dried mushrooms. She left them on the doorstep of the fat shop owner. While hiding behind a pine tree she threw a rock at the door so he would open it up. Seeing him stuff those cookies into his drooling mouth made her smile. He ate them down quickly, flashing his crooked yellow teeth."

"His body was discovered the next morning, but the tall stack of papers listing his customers' charges was never found."

"This solution to problems was passed down for over 200 years, the instructions for identifying the mushrooms rewritten many times. In time, it was always used with homemade mushroom soup. The copy that I have is very old."

I noticed Grace was loving this story. Her bright blue pants suit brought out her beautiful eyes and their expression had changed from sadness to excitement.

After a few minutes passed she asked, "Well, was it used again?"

CHAPTER THIRTY-ONE

I hesitated, saying that I did not know about other times the mushrooms had been used, but I did know that supposedly every woman through those generations had passed down the information.

"Grace, like many family stories, there are holes in the timeline that I have no information about. I could guess there might have been untold accounts, but none of my grandmothers took the knowledge to their grave. Supposedly, it was always retold to some other family female. The next time I have any information about this subject was only guesswork on Grandma Frances' part."

"I spent a lot of time with her when I was a child. She loved to tell stories about the past. I only wish I had written it all down. Children never think of that of course. When it came to the mushrooms, she knew her own mother, Belle, kept them. In those days there were natural methods to deal with almost everything. She passed the soup recipe and legend along to her daughters."

"Do you remember when I told you about Arthur being found dead? Belle had loved him with all her heart, but as he got older, alcohol became his master. Once he was caught by the owner of the local tavern while stealing a bottle from behind the counter. This became gossip all over town, and Belle felt shame. When she ventured out to church or to shop, she knew she was being talked about."

"Belle had endured being poor, having to work hard, and even feeling the heavy guilt of knowing that it was her fault poor baby Aaron died. However, she got to the place that Arthur was more of a liability than the handsome husband she once knew. Whenever she was able to save a nest egg of money, he always found it and bought cheap whiskey. In the autumn of that year, Belle began to see her only escape."

"Now, remember that much of this is speculation from my grandmother. She told me many stories I did not know for sure that I could believe. One of her favorite revenge stories was about a distant cousin named Alfie who supposedly poisoned some of Henry's horses. No matter how much time passed, she was always plotting a way to make him pay. If she made mushroom soup for this guy, I never knew."

"So, I am not totally sure if what she suspected might have happened to her drunken father was fact. She was convinced that Belle, her mother, had fed him a good dose of mushrooms one winter day. They found him almost frozen to the ground in an alley, so maybe he was just a fallen drunk. Nobody in those days would question any of that."

All this time I had been driving, so I could not see the expression on Grace's face, but I did hear her make little sounds. I pulled off I-69 to fill the car with gas, and Grace slowly walked inside to use the restroom. She was mainly only using her cane now. I went inside and ordered a foamy vanilla latte to take along. I did not want to get sleepy before we got home. I offered to buy her one, but she chose a small cup of diet cola.

"Grace, I can't believe that Easter candy is already out for sale. Did you see it there by the cash register? What do you do for Easter? I know you go to church, and I guess that is one time you would be sure to attend. I haven't gone to Easter services for many years. It never seemed the same after I married David. He said it was just a way for people to show off their expensive clothes."

I launched off into telling her about all the Easters I had fixed baskets for my children, and even recalled some of my former Easter outfits. I loved to describe clothing, and was in the middle of the story about my home-sewn yellow linen coat, lined with a splashy silk print.

"Kate," Grace interrupted, "you never finished telling me about the mushrooms! There must have been other times they were used. When we get home, I want to see that old recipe, and you should show me the tureen. It sounds like an amazing antique."

I was surprised by how fascinated she appeared to be about this old family story. The last part was something I hated to remember, let alone tell.

"Well, Grace, I am not sure about this last story. I can barely remember it. I was a teenager, and I only heard my mother talk about it later. All I know for sure is that one hot summer day we all got very sick. At the time we blamed the flu or food poisoning. It was before we could afford a new refrigerator, so something could have spoiled. It was a few weeks later when my mother suspected our illness was from our drinking water. The water in our well was not safe to drink, so we always filled big glass jars at a friend's house."

"My grandfather, the soft-spoken Henry, had gotten very bad news from the doctor. For several years he had been exposed to a pesticide used on our farm. This was the time when chemicals had just begun to be used for bugs and weeds."

"Purdue University had a program to experiment with these chemicals, and even maintained a test farm near us. They rented my grandpa's farm, too, and paid him to use their new weed control spray. My mother can remember him coming in for supper with white powder all over him. This was even written up in a farm journal with his photo in it."

"Soon he developed lymphoma, a deadly form of cancer. The family doctor sent him for testing, and it was horrible news. There was little to no hope for cancer patients then."

CHAPTER THIRTY-TWO

As I thought back to my hardworking, kind grandfather, tears came to my eyes. He had not deserved this type of death. The physician who told him the diagnosis was blunt and unfeeling in the manner he delivered it. His patients had nothing but good things to say about him, but I had never liked his personality. There should have been a kinder way to deliver such tragic news. Poor Grandpa Henry came home with his head held down. He had been given no hope at all.

If this doctor had delivered the diagnosis in a more humane way, perhaps the next few months would have gone differently.

"Grace," I began, "you have to understand that for over fifty years, my grandparents had been inseparable. It was a huge blow to Henry, hearing he would be dead in just a few months. However, wondering how his precious and so dependent Frances would handle life without him was more than he could stand. He had taken care of her for so long he could not imagine her being able to go on. "

"Again, my mother never had proof of his actions, but she somehow came to the terrible conclusion it had been mushroom-laced drinking water that nearly did all of us in. I remembered the taste of the water was off, and then we had all been so sick. If it hadn't had this awful, tainted smell, we may have drunk a lot more. I shudder to think what would've happened. She never confronted her father with her suspicions."

"When people are facing certain death perhaps they cannot make logical decisions, and I can understand if Henry had come to the conclusion that we should all leave together. Perhaps he meant the water just for himself. I do not know, but my mother swore she could detect the mushroom smell in the water. It could have been a new fluoride treatment in the water that made it have a funny taste."

"My grandfather's long hospital stay and ultimate death did prove to be filled with agony. I will never forget how he suffered. I choose to remember the exceptional man he was for all his good days. He enjoyed watching black and white Westerns, and had dreamed of being a cowboy himself when he was young. When he heard the song Red River Valley tears always rolled down his cheeks. It must have been an important song to him and Frances when they were young."

"As it is with so many young people, I didn't realize all that he was until long after his death. He loved me so much and was patient with my silly ways. I was a selfish teenager and could not see beyond that."

"I can look back now and see his work-hardened hands, knuckles swollen with arthritis, and understand everything much more fully as an adult. I will never know the truth of the water incident, but no matter what, I could never blame this gentle man."

"It had become a ritual every spring to head into the woods and gather mushrooms, but I'm not aware of them being used for anything larger than pesky mice."

"I learned from Frances how to recognize the edible ones, and we did make a lot of soup to serve in the old tureen. It is one of my prized possessions. Knowing it was owned by so many generations of brave women makes it more special. It is a symbol of survival."

"The whole story of the mushrooms was told to me by my grandmother. Since it had been retold so many times, I don't know if it is all true or not. Stories have the tendency to change with repeated telling, so it's whatever one wants to believe, I suppose."

Grace had only one question. "Kate, are you going mushroom hunting this year? It should soon be about the right time."

I couldn't picture this frail lady following me through the woods, but I finally agreed we could go and look in a few days.

I was very glad to arrive back in our town and drop Grace at her apartment. Jack gave her a happy hug, and after I took her bag inside we parted company. The long conversations that had occurred on our trip left me a lot to think about.

The excited dogs danced around me for several minutes. I knew my neighbor took good care of them when it was necessary for me to be gone, but they missed me. I had no sooner put my luggage down when my cell phone began to ring. I fumbled to get it out of my purse, and finally answered.

It was Holly's voice at the other end.

"Mom, are you still traveling with that lady? You promised to let me know. Is everything okay? I don't think you should still be running all over the country. It just isn't safe."

I assured her that I was home, safe and sound.

"Well, that isn't the only reason I called. I thought you might fly down and visit for Easter. It isn't like Dad even knows you are around, anyway. That woman has a husband and children to take care of her, doesn't she?"

I tried to explain that I thought of Grace as a friend, and she was definitely not a burden. If Holly hadn't been set on living so far away, she and I could spend time together. Even as a child she had been ambitious and smart. I was not surprised when she announced her need for the move.

David had always taken her side in everything, and I was used to being on the wrong side of any discussion. I adored my daughter, but absence had widened the gap between us. These were her career days and she had made a large circle of friends and business associates. I was her mother, but she sounded impatient and busy when I called.

Holly's call, let alone the invitation, was a nice surprise. I told her I would try to come. Explaining I had just walked in the door, I promised to call back the next day. Something didn't feel quite right, and I wanted to think about it.

It wasn't long before my phone rang again. I was excited to hear Gordon's voice. He got right to the point.

"Kate, I miss you so much. Can I come over?"

CHAPTER THIRTY-THREE

I quickly pulled my thoughts together and replied, "Oh, of course! I have been on a little trip, but I am home now. It will be nice to see you."

Gordon said he would be heading my way soon, then hung up. I quickly re-applied makeup and fluffed up my hair. Glancing into the bathroom mirror, I noticed how tired I looked. The past year had taken a lot out of me. My eyes didn't have much shine left in them. No makeup in the world could fix this.

I barely had time to engage in my usual obsessive worrying about how I would be perceived when the doorbell rang. I pulled open the door to see a noticeably thinner Gordon standing there. It was obvious he had been through a lot since I had seen him. He gave me a little hug. It felt like the way someone reaches out to others when they themselves are hungry for comfort.

I patted his shoulder and motioned to the couch. I shooed the dogs away because they were dancing around looking for attention. They seemed to remember this quiet man. I offered to make coffee, and I was glad he wanted some because it gave me a way to lessen the tension I was feeling.

I wasn't expecting to be nervous, but barely felt it when I burned my hand on the coffee pot. Gordon was petting the dogs and did not notice. I had been making forced small talk but after

I sat down with the coffee cups, I switched to a more solemn tone. I focused my eyes on the rising steam from my best china cups instead of looking him in the face. It had only been a few weeks, but I suddenly thought this was so very awkward.

"Gordon, I can only imagine how stressful this time has been for you. I am so sorry."

"Kate, I'm the one who should be apologizing because I haven't called. I was exhausted when I have had any free time. At the beginning, there was so much to do. Planning a funeral service is so much more involved than most folks realize until they are the one having to do it. As much as I appreciated it, there was an endless line of people who came to comfort me. Over and over, I had to speak to all of them. The funeral director kept asking me questions. I had to make so many decisions."

"It all seemed so surreal. I thought I was prepared to let Mary Anne go, but it was like she died twice. I hated seeing her in the condition she had remained in for so long, but accepting her death was taking it all to a different level."

I told him about the funeral I had just witnessed with Grace and explained how unsettling it had been for me, even though I didn't know the deceased.

"Kate, combined with the grief and sadness, it seemed to go on forever. People volunteered to help in many ways, but at a point, one really does not want a lot of others around. While my son was home I needed to go through a lot of things, and that was harder than I could have imagined. He wanted a few keepsakes that had belonged to his mother, but we also had to sort out so much else. I had avoided even removing her toiletries from the bathroom cabinet. Having to throw away a half-used bottle of lotion she had probably applied just before the accident was enough to make me weep. It was endless."

"I remember when I had helped clean out her mother's apartment, and watching the tears fall as she did this sad task. However, I never understood before now. It was like she had just left and might want to use these items again. I know how crazy this sounds, but letting her everyday things go to the dumpster was the most horrible experience."

"Later on, when I was alone, I realized that every family I had seen lose a loved one would have had to go through this. I hated having to notify family members when I lost a patient, but I suppose it never really hit home until now."

I refilled our cups and felt tears spring to my eyes. We sat and talked for a long time. It was obvious Gordon needed to share his feelings with someone. He recounted the many papers he was forced to sign, and how it had all seemed so final. He also spoke of happier times he had shared with Mary Anne.

His stress seemed to slowly lift as he continued. I suggested eating something, but I hadn't had time to do any grocery shopping. I ended up making tuna salad and baking some croissants from the freezer. We sat in silence as we ate.

I sensed he was preparing to say something. There was a slightly different tone to his voice when he turned to me and spoke.

"Kate, I am not a game player and I like to be honest with everyone. I am so very happy that I met you, and just being here this afternoon has been so very nice. However, I need some time before I can close the door and start off into another phase of my life. I hope that you understand."

"Oh, Gordon, I totally understand. I know that David is never going to recover, but I am his wife. Many times it hasn't been easy, but I have a responsibility to him."

"Kate, please understand I am hoping to spend time with you, and that is important to me. But it will have to be a slow process."

We looked into each other's eyes with total understanding. This was the way it would be staying for a while.

When Gordon gave me a little kiss on the cheek and left, I felt shell-shocked. I carried our dishes to the sink and took care of the dogs. I was strangely content to just let things progress without trying to micromanage every moment of my life.

CHAPTER THIRTY-FOUR

When I woke up the following morning, I lingered in bed for a few minutes replaying all of the events of the past few months. There had been so much drama that I realized I needed to take a break from it all. Last autumn seemed to have happened a very long time ago. The dogs whined to be let out, so I got up and opened the patio door.

It was an unusually lovely warm day and it made me smile to see my furry babies take a whiff of the air and run around in pleasure. On those cold and disagreeable days, they had not lingered outside. I felt somewhat at peace today, and it seemed like a good day to let many things go, including the gray days of winter.

Knowing she would be expecting to hear from me, I gave Grace a quick call. I did not mention Gordon's visit. I told her I was going to start some Spring cleaning and might be busy for a week or so. Her silence made me think she was disappointed, but she said nothing. I knew that having me in her life had created something for her to look forward to, but perhaps it was time to back off a little, anyway.

There was a nice teenager who lived on our street, and I walked down and knocked on her door. I could see the surprised look on her mother's face when she came to the door. It was no longer the world when neighbors just dropped in.

"Hello, Linda," I said. "I was wondering if Marci would be available to work for me, doing some cleaning and so on. I just need a little help."

I was invited to step in and Marci soon appeared. I had bought Girl Scout cookies from her a couple of years ago, and she always seemed like a sweet girl. I secretly thought she looked like a Scandinavian milkmaid, with a fresh pink-cheeked complexion, blonde curly hair, and huge blue eyes.

I explained my need for a part-time helper and mentioned an hourly sum I could pay. She readily agreed, and we decided to start in two days, on Saturday morning.

When I returned home, I made a list of tasks I wanted to complete. It was always difficult for me to make myself start big projects, but if I had a helper, it would be easier. I made a cup of tea and took my notepad out to sit on the patio. The warm sunshine was comforting. I noted that the white wicker patio furniture would need a good cleaning.

I could not help remembering that David had hated this furniture and wanted to buy something more "sturdy." This was one of the things I had made sure to bring along from the big home I had left.

Thinking now of David, I also remembered there were several cartons of his things I had stacked in the garage. Eric wanted to go through the small tools before I got rid of them so I had brought several boxes along. I didn't even look into any of them. They were just as David had left them a few years ago.

Remembering now all that Gordon had suffered through, I decided it was time to open those boxes. David had never liked me messing with his things and got angry when I ventured into his workshop to even borrow a hammer. When I moved I had bought a simple set of tools that would suffice.

I knew it was time to stop keeping one foot in the past. I had done all I could to be a good wife and mother, but I needed to move on and try to let it all go.

I forced myself to focus on the tasks at hand and enjoy this time of renewal. I looked at the brown, withered plants in my flowerpots and decided that planting some cheerful blooms would elevate my mood. I used to plant several beds of annuals and spent every summer pulling weeds and watering. It was a nice memory but now I was very satisfied to only have those few small pots. Even if we had the usual mornings of late winter frosts, they would be protected there on the patio.

I made a list of other things I would need, from groceries to cleaning supplies, and headed out to the shopping center nearby. I remembered taking a cheerful Holly along on this task many years ago. Eric had usually been off playing with his friends, and David had his own projects. That time with Holly was wonderful, but I knew that little girls grow up and go on with their lives as adults.

At one time I would have filled the car with many varieties of flowers, but I knew I only needed a few kinds now. I picked out bright pink geraniums and white petunias. At the last moment I added a small pot of Gerber daisies, because Holly favored these. I tossed in a new pair of floral print gardening gloves and smiled.

It had taken me a long time to realize that I should not buy very many groceries at one time. The years of over-filled carts were also in the past. I carefully put the items from my list into the shopping cart and resisted the temptation to buy other treats. I picked out a couple bags of healthy doggie treats, and was soon heading home.

It was not quite past the season of chilly evenings, so I quickly unpacked my purchases and decided I had made a good start. There was no longer a husband there to make a remark about my quitting early. I had to stop thinking about the years during which I made endless excuses for almost everything.

On impulse I had bought a flat bowl of daffodils, and I put

it out on the kitchen counter. Sitting down at the small white table, I faced the West windows where I could see the amazing spring sunset. Moving the daffodils to the center of the table was a calming decision.

I made a cup of citrus herbal tea, a bowl of soup, and some rye toast. I slowly ate this evening meal, feeling relaxed.

It was a couple of hours later when it occurred to me I should have gone by to look in on David.

CHAPTER THIRTY-FIVE

Friday morning arrived with one of our expected spring rains. I was forced to cancel any outside work and concentrated on indoor tasks. I ate some oatmeal and lingered over my vanilla flavored coffee. There did not seem to be any real reason to rush into anything today. I thought back to other rainy weekends. I always wanted to laze about in bed and have a cozy time with David. He did not have to work on Saturdays, but always managed to find some reason to get up and leave.

I had a preconceived notion of enjoying easy conversations with my husband like two best friends would do. This seemed to be the normal expectation of a marriage. In all those years, we never did this. It was just not in David's playbook. In the beginning I tried to explain why this was important to me, but the usual result was an argument.

"Damn it Kate, I have things to do and you need to get busy, too. I promised my buddy, Larry, that I would go over to his house and help him install some shelves in the basement. I can't lie around all day and talk about nothing. What is the matter with you?"

After hearing things like this so many times I finally gave up. I never fully understood his point of view, but much of our marriage was good. We had a nice home, friends, and I had financial security. David never tired of pointing out how lucky I was.

On this rainy morning much of it came back to me. I don't even know how I had started down this road of memories. I tried to read a book, but soon lost interest. I just finished getting dressed when my phone rang. I wasn't really surprised to hear Grace on the line.

"Honey, this is just such a gray day. I hate to bother you, but would you like to come over? We could have lunch in the big dining room."

I wasn't really planning on getting out in the rain, but something told me that staying home would only provide a long, depressing day. I promised to call back later when my plans were complete. I knew I should stop by and see David, but I eased my guilt by making a phone call. When I spoke to the main nurse on his unit, she assured me he was about the same.

"Mrs. Williams, I know how you feel. We have other spouses who are in the same situation. As you know, your husband no longer remembers his life with you. We can have short conversations with him, and his caseworker asks him questions and shows him photos. However, he is just in his own world now. It is not unusual."

I thanked her for her candor, and felt somewhat like a child who had just heard their school was closed for a snow day.

Every day I felt a mixture of guilt in being glad he wasn't at home anymore, and one of duty in being a wife, no matter what. I also felt regret that I never figured out how to make our marriage more normal. I had observed so many couples that seemed to enjoy being together.

The absence of having a loving father created a constant gap in my life. I constantly was reminded of this when I was a child, and to be honest, I don't think it ever went away. However, by the time I graduated from high school and started college, I thought my life was on the path I wanted it to be. I had a steady boyfriend, a career I wanted to pursue, and could only picture a rich, full future.

But I was still haunted by old insecurities. This put me off my original career path and drove my boyfriend away. For years, I blamed him, but it was all my own doing. I constantly worried everyone in my life would leave me and I would be alone. It was a very real fear to me, and ironically, it made me push people away.

I first met David when I was in school, but he wasn't another student. He was my very young journalism professor. He arrived at our school newly graduated from college himself and soon became the "coolest" professor.

I did not like his method of teaching. He gave me disapproving scowls. I didn't appear to adore him like so many of the other kids. In fact, it made me angry to see him becoming so friendly with them.

He seemed to be a haunted young man. I never gave him a second thought after I graduated until we ran into each other one day.

I was sitting at an outdoor café eating a ham sandwich, and reading the latest best seller. I was absorbed in the book and did not see David approach my table. He said "Hello, Kate," and I looked up with a start. We chatted for a minute or so and I gave him one of my new business cards. I was proud of this achievement and it was suddenly important for me to make sure this impossible man knew about it. I wanted to impress him. I wanted him to like me.

Much later, I wanted him to love me. I suppose that on some level, he did love me, but had no clue about how to express it.

I had walked into his classroom all those years ago and felt a mixture of emotions. He was the kind of man who could not be ignored. He drew young people to him. His angular face could easily smile for some, and scowl for others.

We disagreed on my work, and I soon figured out he did

not really care for my opinion. His gaze made me uncomfortable from the first day. I later realized that I wanted him to like me and act the way I saw him interact with others. He asked what I was reading, and I volunteered how much I wanted to see the movie when it was out.

A few days later I was shocked to hear his voice when I answered my phone.

"Kate, that flick you wanted to see is going to be in the theaters next weekend. Would you like to go and see it with me?"

It was almost like listening to someone else's voice say that I would love to go. He asked where I was living, and we agreed on a time. My head was reeling, but I felt like I was being drawn into a storm — it was both exciting and scary.

I was still living at home, so I walked into the kitchen and told my mother about the phone call. My still-beautiful mother gave me a dubious look.

"Kate, I thought you didn't like this man. I have only met him at a few functions, but he always seemed a little off. It was like he was trying too hard, and almost acting how he thought he should be. Are you sure you want to do this?"

I was young and admittedly did not think very far ahead at the time. It seemed fine for me to go out with David, and I told my mother it was what I wanted to do. The fact she expressed doubt made me even more determined.

Looking back to that date, I don't even recall very much. The only two things I still remember is that he was an hour late, and when he brought me home he leaned over and kissed me. Little did I realize that this kiss changed the course of the remainder of my life.

CHAPTER THIRTY SIX

The sound of my phone ringing brought me back to the present. My daughter wanted to know if I was planning to take her up on an Easter visit. I sighed and said to myself that it might be the perfect thing to do. She was insisting that I plan on flying down for a few days. However, a different plan came to mind.

"Honey, I think that I might just drive down, stay with you first, and then go on down the coast to visit my cousin Val. I can take my time and bring the dogs along. I don't want to leave them again so soon."

I could practically hear my daughter's disapproval. I knew she wasn't all that keen on Mollie and Daisy being in her tidy home.

"Don't worry honey, there are lots of motels that take pets these days. I will stay in one of them, and we can just visit later. I never drive if I get tired, so if it takes me three days to get down there, so be it."

"It is such a shame about Dad. It should be both of you coming to see me."

Holly was always honest and frequently blunt when stating her opinion, so the remark did not surprise me. Her business success was largely based on her ability to address situations head-on, without pretense. I had learned to hide how much her boldness could hurt my feelings. I was never sure if one inherited personalities or just copied what they witnessed as children. She reminded me of David sometimes, but I also could recognize many of my own traits in her.

I went on discussing the practical aspects of the trip and could tell she was smiling by the end of the conversation. I still thought of Holly as my innocent, sweet child, though some negative life experiences had left emotional scars. Her husband Alan adores her and they share the same attitudes about nearly everything.

She and I always found common ground in spending time together, now more difficult at a distance. We both like to haunt estate sales and antique stores. I didn't buy much anymore, but I still like to go shopping. It had been quite a while since we had spent any quality time together, so I vowed to be agreeable to any plans she might suggest. She may not realize until much later how precious times like this can be. It was only when I lost my own mother that I realized how the days of our lives fly by and change. Gordon had mentioned this to me when he was talking about Mary Ann's death.

This thought made me realize that I should call Gordon and tell him about my trip. I was dreading telling Grace, of course. It kind of bothered me that she was seemingly so involved in my life. I enjoyed spending time with her and thought of her as a good friend; however, I did not feel comfortable with the obligation I was sensing. I felt guilty about this, but wanted to take a step back. I had shared information with her that very few people knew. I had to wonder if I would ever regret doing this. I recalled sharing intimate information with a few folks in the past and later discovered that they were not the trusted friends that I had assumed.

Friday sped by, and I knew I would have a busy day on Saturday working with Marci. I decided to put off calling Gordon for a few days. I told Grace I was simply too busy to leave the house.

As expected, Marci did arrive early and I outlined the things I wanted to accomplish that day. She's a happy person, and we chatted about school things and her recent shopping trip to the mall. I enjoyed listening to her, and it made the work go by quickly. The porch was soon clean and inviting for the coming warm months. We mostly concentrated on basic housecleaning. However, by mid-afternoon, I remembered I really wanted to go through the boxes of David's things in the garage.

It was sad to see the tools he had used so often, but I made a box of items to give to Eric. If he didn't want them, he could give them away. At the back of one shelf, there was a deep sealed box I didn't even recall seeing during the move. It looked like it hadn't been opened for some time. I put Marci to cleaning the garage windows while I ripped the tape off the box. In the top I found some papers and items that had been in his school office. There was an address book and other desk accessories.

As I took these things out I discovered a carefully construct-ed false bottom to the box. I slowly pried it up and found a bundle of letters tied with a blue string. I knew I had never seen these before, and David had hidden them on purpose. I was curious, but Marci was asking me a question, so I set them aside for now. We had stopped to eat a little lunch of chicken sand-wiches and fruit. But teenagers are always hungry and Marci wanted to know if she could take a break and snack on cookies she had brought along. I looked around and decided we had done enough for this one day. I paid her for the work, even adding in a little tip. I wanted her to come again.

She had no sooner walked out the door that I heard the phone. I was not surprised to hear Grace's voice. I knew she was curious as to what I had been doing. I looked up at the clock and realized it was now evening. I found myself hungry, so I suggested I come and pick her and Jack up to go out for supper. I knew I was only deepening our connection, but I was tired of eating alone. I quickly changed into a pair of khaki pants and white blouse. I find restaurants cold, so I added a bright red sweater. I began to compose the way I would explain my upcoming journey.

CHAPTER THIRTY-SEVEN

I was actually glad to get out of the house. If I had stayed home I would have come up with many reasons that I should not drive to Florida. David always accused me of overthinking everything. I had to admit that this was true. I went by and picked up Grace and Jack. As always, she looked stunning in a pale pink outfit with a pastel floral scarf. Jack smiled as he got into the car, and I thought he was happy to see me also. It occurred to me that it was unusual for him join into our conversations, except for a word or two.

We decided on a new Italian restaurant, and I realized I had worked up an appetite working all day with Marci. On the drive, we made polite conversation about the weather.

After we were seated and placed our order, I decided that I might as well launch into telling them about my trip. I outlined my conversation with Holly and added in how much I would miss them for a week or so. Jack just smiled but I could tell Grace was not pleased.

"Kate, it seems really dangerous for you to drive all of that way alone. Besides, you'll be missing the best part of spring in Indiana. Everything will be blooming. I was really looking forward to our trip to the woods for mushrooms, too."

I tried to picture how this frail woman could go traipsing

through the trees, but I knew I needed to reply.

"Grace, maybe we could drive out to the state park tomorrow. It would be easier for you to walk there. I am never sure where we might find mushrooms, but we could look."

I could tell this was not really helping, and she still looked out of sorts. However, she seemed to regain her good mood and agreed. I thought that Jack looked relieved when his wife smiled again. Just before our meals arrived, Grace took a plastic pill sorter out of her handbag and gave Jack several different types of meds. He frowned, but she gave him a look, and he dutifully swallowed them. I wanted to ask what he had to take, but this seemed too personal. She mentioned doing his insulin injection later.

When I saw Grace daintily eat spaghetti dripping with sauce, I was amazed her spotless pink jacket did not get a drop of marinara somewhere. I enjoyed my manicotti with a salad and felt satisfied. I rarely let myself eat like this anymore, and it was a treat. Jack ate in silence. We declined desserts and left for home. I sensed a subtle change in Grace, but could not quite pinpoint what was going on with her. I said I would come and get her on the following day, even though I really did not want to. For one thing, I had lots of things to do before leaving, and I had a strange feeling about this outing.

By the time I pulled into the garage I was ready to watch a little television and go to bed. Upon seeing the clean garage I remembered finding that little packet of letters. David was never a fan of writing, so I was guessing they might be thank you messages from former students. I picked up the bundle from the workbench where I had thrown them and went inside. I made a cup of herbal tea and put on my pajamas. There was a classic mystery movie on, and I was ready to stop thinking for a while.

CHAPTER THIRTY-EIGHT

I took a sip of tea and untied the letters. I noticed the post-marks were from quite a few years ago, and they all seemed to be in the same handwriting. I selected one, and pulled the paper out. I expected to find something boring. As I began to read, I found the contents to be anything but. I read the first page and felt a wave of nausea before starting the second.

"Dearest David, I write this again to you, feeling the depths of despair. I miss you so much. I understand how you had to make a big choice for your life. However, it seems so unfair to me, and yes, to you, also. Your last letter to me was so full of sadness and even anger. I think that it is also unfair to Kate. She married you thinking you loved her and wanted to spend your life with her. I almost feel sorry for her, except she is there with you every day. If you ever change your mind, I will be waiting for you to come back to me. I know that we can never really be together, but a few stolen moments would be something. Please call or write when you can. Forever, M"

At this point, I think I went into some type of sickened shock. I sat and did not move, shaking my head. I heard a piti-ful scream and realized it had come from me. I ran to the bath-room and threw up that delicious manicotti dinner. Tears were streaming down my cheeks as I sank onto the cold tile floor.

I grabbed a washcloth and covered my face with it. I held it tightly, wanting to shut out the world. The dogs came in and nuzzled me, wondering what was wrong with their mom.

I lost track of time, but after a while I struggled to my feet and went back to the living room. I knew I had to read all the letters despite the shock and pain they had suddenly caused. I wished I had never opened that box. They had been so close by, hidden all of that time. For years I had gone about my life in blissful ignorance. Granted, David had been thoughtless a lot of the time, and we didn't see eye to eye on many issues, but it had never occurred to me he really did not love me. I had to read the letters, because, if for no other reason, I had to know why everything had happened.

I forced myself to remain calm as I gathered up the letters. I put them in order of date and read from the beginning. The first one was mailed in the first year of my marriage, and they continued at different intervals for over ten years. The same degree of intimacy and hopeless love was the theme in almost all of them, but references to many other events were included. Holidays were mentioned. There were even a few birthday and Christmas cards. The births of our children were discussed. Questions that had to have been posed by David, writing back to "M," were answered. The writer showed scorn for many things that had happened, saying it was impossible for David to have really enjoyed any of it.

By this time I was numb, on autopilot, and looking for information. The letters had a Florida postmark, but it was a large city and offered no clues. There was no return address, nor were names mentioned. They had been mailed to a post office box I had no knowledge of. It appeared that David and this faceless, nameless person had been colleagues or friends at school. Even those casual comments were vague. I had hoped for a way to identify the writer, but nothing was clear. However, just before the letters stopped, it appeared that the writer had some type of medical issue. The handwriting had slowly changed, with the last letters written in a shaky way.

I had to wonder if this person had died. Going by the date of the last letter, I tried to think of what was going on in our lives at that time. It was the summer that Eric had broken his arm and needed a lot of extra attention. I did recall that David failed to display much sympathy for his son, and most of his care fell to me. David rarely shirked his fatherly duties, but I could not remember much from that long ago. I got out old photos and searched for that year. Looking at the expressions on David's face, I actually could see sadness. I also was reminded this had been the summer he had to go and help his brother for a few weeks with a garage he was building. Before his death, his brother had lived in Florida. Had David really gone to visit his secret lover?

CHAPTER THIRTY-NINE

The following morning was every bit the perfect Indiana spring day. The sun rose on dewy rose bushes which were just beginning to show some buds. A dozen twittering birds appeared at the bird feeder Marci had filled for me. That seemed so long ago now. Most of me wished I had never found that packet of letters. Why did this have to happen now? I had promised to take Grace to the park today but I didn't want to be around her yet. She was very perceptive, and I did not think I could come off as my normal self. I hadn't slept much, and I looked older as I confronted the bathroom mirror. Yesterday's mascara was smeared around my eyes. I was pretty sure all of the skin on my face was sagging. I am usually careful to remove my makeup before retiring for the night, but it had been far from my mind.

So many thoughts crowded my mind, fighting for space in my brain. There were so many unanswered questions. If David loved another woman, why on earth had he married me? I tried to imagine what "M" might be like, which was, of course, impossible. There was really no feasible way to look for her. This had been years ago. It did make me realize why David treated me with so much indifference. He didn't want to be married to me. I felt stupid and violated. I wanted to visit Pine Haven and scream at him, demanding answers. If only I had discovered the letters before he became incapable of providing the truth. How could I ever have peace of mind? I felt ashamed and duped and as much as I needed to talk about this, whom could I tell? Certainly not my children. There was no reason to make them aware of this. It would serve no purpose.

Grace had become my confidant in most things. I also considered telling Gordon, but I did not feel comfortable in doing that. All my other friends were not that close any more. I felt more alone than ever. After carefully thinking it through, I decided to confide in Grace. In recent weeks I had come to wonder a little about this sweet little old lady. After she had told me about the fire, it remained shocking to me. I totally understood how horrible that childhood must have been for her, but her role in changing everything was unforgettable.

I also realized that many of her stories were still unfinished. What had happened to her first husband? How had she finally married Jack? There was a lot of her life we had not spoken about. I had been so tied up with the present that I had ignored a lot of the past. There was still much of my life I had not shared, either.

I came to the realization that I could not really hide my emotional upheaval from Grace, so I might as well tell her about the letters. She was expecting me to take her to the park today, anyway. Trying to keep my voice as normal as I could, I called her. I arranged to pick her up right after she and Jack ate lunch. I had no appetite, but knew I should make myself a light breakfast. I substituted tea for my usual coffee and made toast. My stomach was still lurching when I ate the toast, but I ate tiny bites and sipped the tea.

I barely felt like combing my hair and putting on makeup, but I went through the motions. I chose a simple blue shirt and jeans. It was still a little chilly, so I added a lightweight gold cardigan. Since we were supposed to be gathering mushrooms

I picked up a couple of bags. The dogs seemed to sense something was wrong as I petted them goodbye. I gave them a couple of treat bones, thinking I could at least provide them with a good day.

I managed a little smile when Grace appeared in spotless powder blue. We were going to the park and the woods, but I had never actually seen her in casual clothing. I heard myself making small talk as we drove down the street. By now the sun had warmed the car, and I pulled off my sweater when we arrived at the parking area. I helped Grace out of the car and handed her the cane. She rarely used the walker now. There were several benches along the trail, so I was pretty sure she would be okay.

"Honey, I so very much appreciate your doing this!" purred Grace. She was obviously very excited and chatted on about the beauty of the flowers and the fragrance of the tree blossoms. I was glad I did not have to struggle to find a subject to discuss. We walked slowly to one of the trails and she started asking me questions about species of mushrooms. It actually did not take long to spot some of the delicious morels our area was known for. I carefully picked them and put them into one of the bags. Grace did not leave the trail, but pointed to various places she thought I should check out.

"Show me the poison ones, Kate! I want to be sure to see what they look like. I have some evidence of mouse droppings around our apartment, so I want to get a supply of those."

I was a little horrified to hear her glee about the prospect of poisoning mice. Soon I spied the ones that supposedly produced a powerful dose of death. I hadn't dried these for a long time, even though I still had a little jar of that deadly powder. I could recall my grandmother making sure there was a good supply in her cabinet. But I really did not remember her killing a lot of mice, even though she told me that she always wanted to have it on hand.

I showed them to Grace and put several into the other bag. I had been cautioned many times about taking care to isolate the Death Cap. Grace stopped to rest on one of the little benches, however I continued on for a while, carefully scanning the woods. I was rewarded by finding a few more morels, which Grace had said she was really craving. After putting more mushrooms into both bags, I suggested it was time to go. By the time we reached the car, Grace was pleading for me to fry some morels for her.

"Please, Kate," she said, "can't we go to your house and have some of these? Jack has some sports thing he is watching today, and he doesn't even like them."

Knowing that I still wanted to tell her about the letters, I agreed. On the way I retold the story of my great, great grandmother making the mushroom soup for the Yankees. Nobody had ever openly said that she poisoned them and had somehow disposed of their bodies, but that was the impression I was always given. Grandma Frances had alluded to a couple more times that she was pretty sure they were used, but I never knew how much was true.

I could tell Grace was tired when we reached my home, but she enjoyed sitting on the couch with the dogs while I breaded the morels and put them in the skillet. I also made iced tea. It had turned into a fairly warm day, and we were thirsty. Grace asked to see the already dried poison mushrooms, so I showed her the little jar that I kept far up in the cabinet. She sniffed it with interest, and sat down at the table to enjoy the morels. I filled large glasses with tea and put out two small plates. Just as I was putting the platter of fried mushrooms at the center of the table, Grace knocked over my tea, sending it splashing onto my clothing. She apologized immediately, but I assured her this was an old outfit, so no worries.

I excused myself for a few minutes to change into dry clothing. When I returned she was daintily sipping her tea and nibbling on a crisp morel. I thought it was time to tell her about the letters.

CHAPTER FORTY

S ince we had been discussing that long ago mushroom
soup that was served to the Yankees, I carefully got out
the porcelain tureen with violets on it. I always marveled
it had survived all these years. I hoped that Holly would want
to take it at some point. It was so much more than an antique,
or even just a family heirloom. It came with a rich history and a
legend. I set it down carefully for Grace to see, and told her how
much it meant to me. After talking about the tureen for a bit,
I put it back into my maple hutch and sat down at the table.

I took a deep breath and said, "Grace, I have something to
tell you about. I have been hiding my emotions from you all
day, but I just have to talk about it."

The old lady gave me a sharp look with a furrowed brow,
and I could tell she wanted to know almost everything about
my life. I hardly knew where to begin.

"Grace, you know how I've told you that I have never understood why David was so distant in our marriage. I had my feelings hurt so many times. I must have tried to talk to him thousands of times, trying to understand why he showed this attitude
to me. But we never had an honest and open conversation."

"So many times I tried to be the woman he expected and
do whatever I could to make us into a happy, close couple.

Oh sure, we did things together, and reared our children. We met problems together and went about the tasks of just living. However, in the back on my mind, I missed the relationship I envied in others. At some point I was happy to see him drive away for errands or whatever, because he always seemed more congenial when he came back."

"Kate, I'm not sure how you endured this for so very long. I have loved Jack for a long time, but I would never put up with him if he caused me to be unhappy."

Grace paused and gave me a little smile, "Kate, you know all of those pills I give to Jack? I learned a while back that it just works best for him to be calm and a little sleepy. I found a supplement at a health food store that helps make him this way. I add it in with his blood pressure medicine and he never thinks a thing about it. When I am gone I put out his pills so he continues to take them regularly. Even though we truly love each other, he got a little mouthy in middle age, so I had to find a way to shut that off."

I paused, stunned by Grace's revelation. For a moment I had second thoughts about telling her the story of finding the letters. However, I simply had to tell someone, and she was the obvious choice.

"Grace, I found something yesterday that is totally devastating to me and I have to tell you."

I related the way Marci and I had been cleaning and the discovery of the letters. I even let her read one of them. I hoped she would make me feel better. As she read, I held my breath, not knowing what she would say. When she finally looked up I could see anger sparkling in her blue eyes.

"Kate, I am so sorry. You lived all of your life with a lying bastard. I suppose it is a good thing you never knew a long time ago, but this makes me very angry. What kind of man leaves the person he loves and marries another woman? This is crazy!"

"That is the main reason I am so upset. It is way too late to even find out who this person is. Since the letters stop abruptly, maybe she died. She could have found someone else and broken it off. There could have been a final letter and David destroyed it. I will never know. It is a terrible mystery. I wish I could know all the details."

Grace had a strange, terrifying look on her face. She looked even angrier than I was. I waited for her to say something.

"Kate, you have a good man now. Divorce David and have a good rest of your life with Gordon. You deserve it."

I had actually thought about this the previous night, but I knew it was a bad idea. Eric and Holly would never understand, and there would be financial problems. Because he needed constant care, David's money would be tied up and I would not even get the pension money I lived on now. I explained to Grace why divorce was not an option.

Grace thoughtfully nodded her head and said nothing. I sensed it was time for this day to come to a close. I changed the subject to my upcoming trip to Florida, and was surprised when Grace said what a good idea it was for me to go. I sent some of the fried morels home with her, saying she could warm them up later. I promised to call soon when I saw her into the apartment.

On the way home my phone rang. I pushed the Bluetooth connection on the steering wheel and was pleased to hear Gordon's voice. This also reminded me I needed to tell him about my trip. He sounded tired, but I readily agreed to have a late supper with him. I realized I had barely eaten in the last 24 hours and was feeling really run down. He said he would pick me up in just a bit. I hurried home and took care of the dogs and changed my clothes. I quickly put on some makeup and tried to arrange my hair. I probably still smelled like someone who had hiked in the woods, but decided not to worry about it.

When I answered the door and saw Gordon standing there, I managed to smile. My smile continued when I saw the car in the driveway. It was the BMW I had thought he was just joking about. He opened the car door for me and it felt good to sink down into the soft leather seat. He asked what I would like to eat. Suddenly, I was so hungry that I knew the answer. I laughed when I told him I needed a giant rare cheeseburger and maybe even some fries. We ended up at the replica 50s diner near the mall.

"Kate, this is really going to derail my diet, you know," Gordon said with a laugh. "I have been trying so hard to lose weight."

"I think you look wonderful just the way you are," I replied, meaning every word.

After we slipped into a booth and gave our order, we just sat and looked at each other for a minute. He seemed as happy to see me as I was to be with him. He related how he had gone about closing his practice and being sure that his long-time patients were referred to other doctors. I told him about doing the house cleaning with Marci and hunting morels with Grace.

I jumped right into explaining my Florida trip and noticed some sadness on his face.

"Kate, I will miss you while you are gone. Are you sure it will be a good idea for you to go alone? It's a dangerous world out there."

I said that the dogs were going, which he found amusing.

"I can get you a gun or pepper spray, if you want. I will worry about you."

It was my turn to laugh. "I would not feel right about having a gun, and there isn't enough time to get a permit, anyway. Actually, I DO have pepper spray in the glove compartment. I got it right after David went to Pine Haven. At first, I carried it when I left there after dark. I never felt any danger, so I just left it in the car."

After our burgers arrived we concentrated on eating. I could not believe how hungry I was. At one time I would have been embarrassed to let Gordon or anyone see me with ketchup dripping on the table as I ate greedily. I suddenly realized that the discovery of the letters, despite being shocking, had freed me to just be myself.

I told Gordon the details of my trip and how I was looking forward to seeing Holly. I had also arranged to visit my cousin and another friend. I suddenly realized I should go and see David's sister-in-law, who might be able to shed some light on my mystery.

A look of happiness came over Gordon's face. "Kate, I have a wonderful idea!" I have an old college friend who lives in At-lanta, and I haven't seen him a long time. Why don't I ride along with you that far? He has an enormous house and you can spend the night there before you travel on. I know he and his wife would just love it. You can just pick me up on the way back."

Before the evening ended, we had made a plan. I felt a great weight lift off my mind.

CHAPTER FORTY-ONE

P lans for the Florida trip shifted into high gear. I made one of my famous lists of things to pack, things to do, and things to buy. This was one of my favorite parts of any vacation. As children Holly and Eric usually wanted take along a ton of toys, games, and other odd items. Sometimes I had to veto a few things on their lists.

Thinking back on those long past times was always bitter-sweet, but now I had added thoughts. Was David thinking of his nameless girlfriend when we took those trips? Did he secret-ly send her postcards? After we returned home, did he write to her and say how he wished it had been her who went with him? I tried to control these thoughts because I felt myself starting to descend into a deep pit of sadness, and yes, even hate. I knew there would be no coming back from all this emotion.

I tried to realize it was probably a good thing I had lived through all those years with no clue about the real David. I always felt sad and confused when he showed me very little warmth or closeness. I had expected marriage would bring that into my life. I do not know if I could have stayed around if I had known he secretly loved someone else for all of that time.

The most difficult part of preparing to drive south with Gordon was the visit I had to pay to Pine Haven. I steeled myself when I entered David's room. He turned to face me with the blank look I had now become accustomed to seeing. He evidently thought I was an employee of the facility and complained about his breakfast. I said nothing. Part of me wanted to pick up the bedside lamp and smash him over the head with it. I now found it very difficult to summon up much compassion for this man with whom I had shared almost all of my life.

David went back to stacking and re-stacking a deck of cards and ignored me standing there. I stood silently for a few more minutes, then gave him one last look before I slowly walked down the hall. It usually bothered me to hear sad sounds from the other patients' rooms. But I heard nothing this morning. I was on another plane of consciousness. I made a quick stop at the nurses' station, telling them I was going out of town. My shoulders sagged as I wondered how I could continue to do this in the coming years. It always had been challenging for me to accept, but now I felt I was responsible for a stranger.

A few days before we left, I stopped by to tell Grace and Jack goodbye and to leave her my travel plans. I was expecting to hear from her before now and was surprised she wasn't chattering away while I stood in their living room. After all this time, I still did not feel like I really knew this woman. The smile plastered on her face seemed somehow forced. I hugged her and said to call me if anything came up.

Gordon tried to get me to agree to driving his big car, but I told him I felt more comfortable in my compact Chevy. I then recalled the years of driving big vans and station wagons when I had a family to take along. How could I have taken all of that for granted?

At this point I was simply annoyed with myself. Get it together, Kate. Stop living in the past. I made a vow to banish these painful thoughts. With a deep breath I decided to only look forward — this was my time. I had no idea what the future held for David, but I had nothing to feel guilty about.

In the early morning sun I gathered up my bags, my dogs,

and other odds and ends I decided to take. I had given Marci a key and she agreed to bring in the paper and the mail while I was gone. I called Gordon and told him I was on the way. He sounded happy and excited. When I saw him standing on the side of the driveway I broke into a grin. The dogs liked to ride in the car and had already settled down in the back seat. They were accepting of Gordon by now and barely gave him a glance.

I felt amazingly free as I drove across the bridge into Kentucky. A couple of hours later we decided to grab breakfast at a fast food place and eat it at a rest stop where we could walk the dogs. We made casual conversation about other vacations we had both taken.

"Gordon," I said, "I'm so glad this worked out for you to go along. I'm sure it would have been okay if I had gone alone, but this is much nicer."

"You know how much I enjoy your company, Kate. You're very accepting and patient when life gets in the way."

I did not even feel guilty about eating a sausage biscuit sandwich and an order of hash browns. Normally I would have ordered yogurt or oatmeal.

I apologized for making him ride in my small economy car, but he assured me he did not care at all. We ate at a picnic table and watched fellow travelers. If I had been alone, some of them might have frightened me. I had been planning to take a big can of roach spray and even considered purchasing a stun gun.

Soon we cleared up our trash and returned to the car. On impulse, I asked Gordon if he would like to drive, and he agreed. We rode along for a short while until I suddenly decided to tell him about the letters. I realized I did not want to lie to this man.

"Gordon, I am sorry to have a serious conversation on such a nice journey, but I want to tell you something." His brow furrowed. I wondered if this was a bad idea. I explained what I had read in the letters and how much they had hurt me. He listened intently until I was finished with the story.

"Gosh, I'm so very sorry that you have had to experience so much pain. But I'll have to admit I feared something much worse. My first thought was that you were going to say we should not be seeing each other. I'm so relieved! You know, I noticed I was actually whistling while I was packing. It came to me that I had not let myself feel that happy in a long time. I'll never forget Mary Anne and what a good life we had, but her accident left me alone and depressed."

CHAPTER FORTY THREE

Hours sped by quickly as we headed south on the crowd-ed interstate. By the time we were winding through the Smokey Mountains in southern Tennessee, both Gordon and I were in high spirits. I found myself wishing he was going to be my companion for the rest of the trip. When we arrived at his friend's home in suburban Atlanta, I felt hap-pier than I had in a very long time. I was given a lovely bed-room for the night, and the Smithsons did not mind the dogs being there at all. Josie was a gracious host with a slow South-ern drawl I found simply charming. Her husband "Pudge" ob-viously adored his old friend Gordon, and they immediately spoke of plans for the next few days.

"Kate, it is so nice to meet you," gushed Josie, nodding her head. I immediately fell in love with their home, built to resem-ble Tara, and I half expected Scarlett O'Hara herself to come tripping down the stairs. Before their retirement, both husband and wife had been doctors, and now in retirement could afford this amazing home.

I suddenly felt exhausted from the long drive, and was even more so after eating the sumptuous meal Josie had prepared. Fried chicken is a staple in the South, and that combined with pan-fried potatoes and sweet buttered cornbread were enough to lull me into a deep sleep. Just before waking up I had the old dream. My children were young again. David was getting dressed for work. I could hear them laughing together.

For just a second, as sunshine streamed through the window, I nearly forgot it wasn't really happening right now. I felt a combination of disappointment and relief to come back to the present. I know I thought I could make things better if only I could re-live those early years.

I heard a soft tap on my door and opened it to find a whispering Josie. She said she would make me breakfast before I left on the second part of my drive. I suggested toast, fruit, and coffee since I needed to be alert. I quickly showered and dressed, because I did need to be on my way. It was nearly 500 more miles to Holly's home and it would be evening by the time I arrived.

I was surprised to hear Pudge and Gordon laughing together in the spacious kitchen. He said he had gotten up early to feed and walk the dogs for me. Part of me really wanted to just stay here with Gordon and these charming hosts, but it was time to go. Gordon walked me out, cautioning me to drive with care. At the last minute he gathered me into a comforting hug and kissed me on the cheek. I wanted to beg him to go with me, but instead I gave him my best smile. The dogs settled down for a nap in the back seat, and I was off.

I hadn't been on the road long when my cell phone rang. Fighting traffic, I was thankful for Bluetooth, and pushed the dashboard connection. At first I thought it might be Gordon, but it turned out to be Grace. She said she just wanted to check on us, and asked where I was. I gave her my location and asked if everything was okay.

"Well, Kate, I thought you might have changed your mind and stayed home. I just wanted to check. I hope you have a wonderful time. Don't worry because everything will be fine here."

I thought this was a strange thing to say, because I had not asked her to check on the house or anything. I supposed that she just wanted to reassure me. We chatted for a few more minutes and I told her how nice it was to have had Gordon along on the first day of driving. I went on to describe the Smithsons' gorgeous home. I was getting into heavier traffic, so I told her I should probably hang up but would let her know when I arrived at Holly's.

It was beautiful weather and I enjoyed taking short breaks at a few rest stops. The dogs excitedly sniffed all the unfamiliar smells and were reluctant to get back into the car. Josie had sent along a couple of sandwiches so that I could avoid looking for fast food. I laughed when I opened the bag and also found a large chunk of Hummingbird cake left over from the previous evening's meal. Oh well, I thought. Vacation food doesn't count.

It wasn't long before I crossed the Florida state line and made the traditional stop at the official welcome center. I have always had a habit of cluttering the car with brochures about the various attractions from the state I was entering. I selected a few, hoping to make a few visits to points of interest. I can recall my children complaining about stopping at some of these so long ago. They just wanted to get to the beach.

It was late afternoon when I drove into Holly's driveway. It was a whimsical older bungalow painted in beach-inspired colors. She had arranged for a few days off from her job while I was visiting, and her husband was out of town on business. After hugs and smiles she helped take my luggage to the spare room. The dogs welcomed being able to explore the fenced back yard. It was planted with tropical foliage and had a charming white fence.

"Holly, I miss seeing you so much. But I know how happy you are living here and how much you love your job." She was the publicist for a large animal sanctuary and enjoyed every minute. For the next few minutes Holly talked about her duties and the animals she was around every day. It was wonderful to see her eyes light up as she spoke.

"Mom, be honest, how is dad? Does he know you're down here? Does he hate being in that place?"

"Holly, I know this is hard to hear, but he doesn't even know who I am now. He complains about the food a lot, but it is really pretty good. I can do no more than see to his care, safety, and comfort."

I opened my mouth to tell her about my relationship with Gordon, which I had not mentioned before. However, I thought better of it. I didn't want to bring anything up that might cause a strained conversation. I had simply told her I dropped off a friend in Atlanta with no further explanation.

"Maybe you can come up for next Christmas and see your father then? But be prepared for him to seem very different."

She changed the subject and said we needed to go out and get some supper. I brought the dogs in and confined them to her laundry room. We weren't sure how well they might get along with her huge orange tomcat.

We got into her bright yellow jeep and she took a shortcut to the nearest Italian restaurant. I took note of her healthy tan and sun-streaked hair, and was happy to see she was thriving here. After we placed our order, I began to tell her about Grace and Jack.

"Well, Mom, I 'm glad you've made some friends. You're taking care of Dad, I know, but you have to think about your own well-being. Of course I miss having days to hang out with you, but this is the life I always dreamed of."

I assured her I understood. We made plans to drive to the beach before dawn the next day. We both loved shelling and beach combing. She had figured out the best places to go and studied the tides. My rule of thumb was to pick up everything, but Holly only took the most beautiful specimens.

After spending the morning finding treasures in the sand, we showered and headed to the big flea market nearby. In earlier days I brought home lots of "finds," but on this day I only purchased a few things. Holly carefully chose a figurine to add to her vintage cat collection.

Later, we took tall glasses of lemonade to her patio to rest and watch the dogs explore. We had carefully avoided speaking of anything controversial today. My daughter now turned to me with sincerity in her big brown eyes, and said, "Mom, I really do know how hard it must be for you now. I just don't know how to help."

"Honey, I don't expect you be able to do anything more than email and talk on the phone. I really am very happy for you. Of course, I would love for you to live 10 minutes away, but if something came up, it's just a short flight back to Indiana."

For the next few days, we shopped, cooked, and laughed together. As hard as it was to drive away, I felt we had taken our mother/daughter relationship to a new and closer place. I noticed tears in her eyes as we hugged goodbye.

CHAPTER FORTY-FOUR

B efore leaving home I had looked up the address and phone number I had for David's brother. I had never been to the home his wife had retired to after becoming a widow. He had passed away many years ago and I wondered if she was still alive. I entered the number, half expecting to find out that it was no longer in service. I was surprised when it began to ring. A soft Southern voice answered and I told her who I was. Millie Mae even had a name that seemed to belong in Florida. We had known each other from previous visits, but were never really close.

I explained I was going to be on a trip near her home and wanted to stop by. She seemed to be accepting of this. I was glad she remembered me. I sped down the western coast of Florida, letting her know my arrival was only minutes away. She lived in one of those little communities with manufactured housing and orange trees. Her children lived in other states, so she was dependent on her friends, just as I was.

I actually did want to visit with Millie Mae, but in the back of mind I thought she might shed some light on my husband's old girlfriend. As painful as it was to think about, I wanted to know more. I was glad I had GPS. The complex she lived in was large with many streets that all looked alike. There was even a small shopping area, community center, and a drug store chain store. I gathered that the older residents never had to leave and could do almost everything right there.

When I finally found the house there was a golf cart in the driveway. I had not seen Millie Mae for years, but should have expected to see how much she had aged. The persistent Florida sun had hardened her skin into golden brown wrinkles, and her iron gray hair seemed thin. She had always been slender, but in old age she looked frail. Her Bermuda shorts hung loosely on her body.

She gave me a big smile and hug and ushered me into her cozy kitchen. A noisy window air conditioner gave the room some cool comfort. It reflected the home of an older person with an array of pill bottles on the counter and aged appliances. She had put out a plate of store bought cookies and there was a pitcher of tea. I hoped this had not strained her budget.

We spoke of old times when we had brought the family to Florida for vacations. She and David's brother lived in a more upscale home back then. She motioned around the room and explained that this was all she required now, and how nice it was to be close to other people.

She brought out faded photos and we let them take us back in time. After a few minutes her expression changed and she spoke in a very quiet voice.

"Kate, I've wanted to call you many times, but just didn't. When I got your last Christmas card updating me about David's condition, I knew it was time to speak up. I don't have no computer or email or anything, so I wasn't sure how to have this long over-due conversation. It was a relief when you phoned to say you were coming." She gestured to the ancient rotary phone hanging on the kitchen wall.

My interest was on high alert now and I wondered what she wanted to tell me. My mouth went dry and I felt a little sick to my stomach, but I hoped she knew the facts about my husband's Florida lover.

"Do you remember when David came down here to stay with us a few times many years ago? You had to work and your kids were little, so it was a good excuse for him to come alone."

"I'm fairly sure you never knew much about your husband. Oh, believe me, he was a darned good man, but he came to regret he had hurried you into a marriage that just wasn't right. He said many times how he felt guilty about it. He wanted to be a good husband and father, but it was hard to do that a lot of the time."

By now, I was feeling faint and strangely hot. I tried to hide it and steadied my hands.

"David met someone he grew to love a few years before you two got married. Even though his job was in Indiana they spent a lot of time together, as much as they could. He seemed so happy when he was down here."

I finally found words to speak. "Millie Mae, I recently found the old letters and it was a shock to me. You know, I sensed he wasn't happy in our marriage, but I never knew there was someone else he really wanted to be with. I simply don't understand why he married me."

"Things weren't that bad when the children were small, but as years passed by, David seemed to become more distant. I felt he was taking out a lot of anger and disappointment on me. I did everything I could to have a close relationship but it never seemed possible."

"Kate, I should have done something to speak to you a long time ago. Forgive me. All these years you tried to do the impossible."

I was riddled with anxiety. "What do you mean?"

"David was working to get tenure in his job, and one day the dean of his school called him into his office. It was explained to him that the governing board of the school only offered tenure to steady family men. It was suggested that getting married and having children would greatly improve his chances. Remember things were different then. So-called "family values" were a big deal to the board of directors in schools."

"He left that office very angry and was set to just resign and move down here to Florida. That happened to be the day he ran into you. Maybe it was meant to be. He told us he almost immediately knew what to do. If more time had passed, I don't know if he would have done it."

My frustration grew. "I still don't understand! Why me?! If he loved someone else, why pull me into a marriage that he did not really want?"

"This was Indiana in the 1960s. He needed to have a solid traditional marriage to keep his position. It was a shame, but it would have been years before he and Michael could have been together and had a real life."

CHAPTER FORTY-FIVE

I had not spoken or moved for a long time. I was frozen in my spindly white chair, listening to the rattle of the old air conditioner and staring at the floral centerpiece. My hostess said no more for a while. She realized she had revealed a long held secret and put me into shock. I suppose my face said it all. After a while, she spoke.

"So you did not know?"

"I... I had been trying to picture some faceless woman who held my husband's heart. Someone who was the cause of so much anger and sadness and feelings of despair. For all those years, I felt that no matter what I did, I was lacking in some unknown wifely skills. It was a daily albatross around my neck. I did love David, you know, but I never could figure out what was wrong."

My mind was racing, remembering so many things that now made sense. Instead of being very close to hating David, I now felt mostly sadness and pity for him. I also realized he could never have found a way to tell me. He was locked into a role he was cast into, and dragging me along was just collateral damage.

One immediate thought was that I could never tell Holly and Eric. It had always saddened them to see their parents at odds with each other so often, but they could live with that. I really wished I could go to my husband and let him know that I basically understood. But part of me would always be angry he could not fathom how he would ruin my life before it was way too late.

Millie Mae had paused for a few minutes while I was taking it all in. She finally began to speak again.

"Kate, I don't really remember a lot of the details, so I can't fill in all the blanks for you. However, I do recall that Michael was sick with something and then was killed in a boating accident a long time ago. I called David at his office to tell him. He did attend the memorial service, and Michael's body was cremated. He had not been in touch with his family for years. I think David told you he had to come help his brother build something."

This was around the time when our old photos reflected an angry look in David's eyes. In his grief he had somehow come to resent having to marry me, and I was the only one around to blame. As years went by we became roommates, struggling to make life work for us and for the children. It was deeply disturbing never being hugged or kissed anymore, but it was obvious he had settled into an accepted life and tried to make the best of it.

Many times he told me how I did not measure up in different ways, but I never really understood until now. I asked a few more questions, but Millie Mae did not remember much more. She thought Michael had visited David in Indiana a few times but had no details. David worked very late a lot of the time, so I would have thought nothing about it. I thanked her and quickly said goodbye. When I had arrived at her little home a few hours ago, I had no idea what I would be learning.

I had planned to drive further south to see my cousin, but I made up a lame excuse and called to say I would not be visiting. Instead I did a phone search for an affordable motel along the coast. I finally found one with a vacancy and gave them my credit card number. I put the address in my GPS and set out.

It was still a couple of days before Gordon was expecting me to pick him back up. I needed some time alone now.

The rundown motel was somewhat disappointing as it was not even near the beach, but I took the room anyway. It looked fairly clean and the front desk person made me feel safe. He was a jolly, balding man who gave me a wide smile. I mentioned the dogs, and he had no problem with that. They had been walked and fed at Millie Mae's house. I stopped at a corner grocery for a loaf of bread, some cheese, and a couple of bottles of water.

I had asked for a non-smoking room but my nose told me this had not always been the case. Normally I would have complained, but I just was careful to keep my clothing in the suitcase. I felt a pounding headache coming on, so I fed the dogs a few treats, took them out for a minute, then ate a small sandwich. A couple of pain pills helped lull me to sleep. I didn't even pull down the faded bedspread.

The next day I woke up way too early but knew it would be impossible to sleep any more. I turned on the dated television and tried to concentrate on a decades old sitcom. I had origi-nally wanted to spend two nights here but it wasn't tolerable, so I checked out and started back north.

By now I knew I would have to tell Gordon what I had learned. I called him and said we needed to go home a day early. For so many months I had avoided visiting David, but I now felt a big need to see him. I didn't know how much time he might have left, but I wanted desperately to tell him I un-derstood. Even though he had caused me many years of frustra-tion, I felt profoundly sorry for him.

Gradually I was finding some peace of mind. They say the truth can set you free and that is seemingly accurate. I thought back over many happenings and wished I could remember more of the first ten years of our marriage. I concluded it was probably best I could not recall all that much. I drove along so lost in thought that the poor dogs had to whine to alert me to their need for a potty break.

Holly called to ask how the rest of my vacation was going. I kept my voice steady and assured her it had been a good idea to come. She said again how much she had enjoyed seeing me. I also called Eric to see if he had any news. He had never held long conversations, so he just said that everything was fine. I called Grace and told her I would be home a day sooner than expected.

"Oh Kate, you should stay as long as you can. Enjoy yourself! Don't come home early."

I wanted to explain, but at that point I wasn't even sure if I was planning to tell her any of the big things I had learned. I felt she would want to talk it to death, and I did not think I could do that.

"Grace, I still have to go back and spend another night at Gordon's friends' home, but we will be home late tomorrow."

She was eager to hang up, so I told her goodbye and concentrated on my driving in the traffic around Atlanta. When Gordon came out to greet me I was happy to see his expression. I had no doubts left that he cared for me. However, as happy as this made me, I felt a huge pang of guilt. My clueless husband was still alive, and I had no idea what would happen in the coming months.

CHAPTER FORTY-SIX

We spent another pleasant evening with the Smithsons, and even with all that was on my mind, it was nice to feel somewhat normal. We thanked them profusely and drove away the next morning. I was again letting Gordon drive. We left before dawn to avoid the morning traffic and chatted along as we left the city. After we were on the interstate heading North, Gordon quietly spoke to me in a different voice.

"Kate, I know you well enough to realize that something is different. Did things not go well with Holly? I am trying not to be nosey, but I hate to see you upset. You don't have to tell me, if you don't want to."

"Oh, I DO want to tell you. I just have to find the right words."

I began my story with an explanation of David's trips to visit his brother. Slowly I worked up to talking about the letters and wondering if Millie Mae might possibly remember something. I was just getting to the place that the startling conversation began when my phone rang. I reached over and tapped the Bluetooth connection and said "Hello."

There was a short pause, and then a deep voice at the other end asked if I was Mrs. Williams. I did not recognize the voice at all, but I replied that I was.

"This is Doctor Abernathy from Pine Haven. I am sorry to have to tell you this, but when the nurse looked in on your husband David this morning she discovered he had evidently passed in his sleep. I understand you are out of town and I dislike having to inform you like this. It has not been unusual for some of our other patients with this cruel disease to pass unexpectedly. I can assure you, Mrs. Williams, that David received excellent care. Nothing could have been done."

Gordon had quickly pulled into a rest area and was sitting quietly, listening with me. I realized I was crying. The last two days had been the most shocking of my life. I could not say a word. Gordon spoke up then, explaining who he was. He and this doctor happened to know each other so it was easy for them to talk. He explained he was driving me home and estimated a time of arrival. I had previously listed emergency information, and David's body was already in route to the funeral home. Long ago he had chosen to be cremated and the doctor assured us that it could be quickly arranged.

I instructed him to wait on that. I wanted to see David one last time. After we hung up, Gordon patiently let me sit there in the car while I gathered myself. He took the dogs for a short walk in the grass and got me a soft drink out of the vending machine. I managed a couple of sips, then went to the restroom.

My mind was spinning again. I knew I had awful calls to make to Holly and Eric. I had to speak to the funeral director and various other people. Gordon offered to help me.

"Kate, you know that I have just been through all of this. I will assist you as much as you want. I don't want to jump in if you don't feel right about it."

"Oh, no, Gordon, I would so appreciate your help. I just don't even know what to do. I just don't know. We really have to get home, though."

For the next few hours we discussed many of the necessary

details as we drove along. I had called my children before leaving the rest area. Holly had broken into tears and asked questions. I wished I could hug her. Her husband was still out of town and she was alone. Her best friend could be counted on to care for the cat, so she said she would be on the next plane. I explained it would still be several hours before I was there. I then realized I had not told her about Gordon.

Eric said he would pick Holly up at the airport and do all that he could to help. I thought about how he had not taken his children to see David for a long time. It didn't really matter now.

I always carried a notebook, so I began a new list. I made a few other calls to folks who would need to know, and decided to tell Grace in person.

I spoke briefly to the funeral director but explained only the basic things David would want. They took care of almost everything. I had long ago written up information that would be needed in both of our obituaries, but it was at home. I promised to get it as soon as I could.

David had a lot of suits, but there would be no showing with cremation. I did not know if I needed to supply clothing or not. The details had never entered my mind before. Gordon jumped into the conversation several times, making the process so much easier.

Holly called both Eric and I with her flight information and I was glad we would be home before her arrival. After what seemed like an eternity we finally crossed the Ohio River and were back in Indiana.

My first stop was at home to release the puzzled dogs. I then quickly told Marci and her mother what was going on. They both expressed sympathy and hugged me. I picked up the obituary information and took it to the funeral home. There were other questions that I had to answer. It was still an hour or so before Holly would arrive.

Gordon suggested we go by Pine Haven to see what was

necessary there. He remembered having to sign papers after Mary Anne passed. It occurred to me what a short time ago that had been. It was overwhelming to just walk in the front door. Gordon took my arm as we approached the nurses station.

The nurses on duty told me as much as was necessary. They were used to giving out bad news. They promised to pack up his things and have them ready for me to pick up. We talked about how hard it was for patients in this wing, and that he had been agitated so much of the time. While they did not exactly call his death a blessing, they implied it. I suppose I thought it was his destiny and likely a peaceful way to go.

As we turned to leave one of the nurses said, "At least he had a wonderful supper. That little old lady brought him a container of delicious smelling soup. She wouldn't even let us have a taste, either. After he ate she insisted on cleaning up for us, the sweet gal. Is she his aunt? I don't think she ever told us."

CHAPTER FORTY-SEVEN

I don't remember much of the next few seconds as the obvious truth swept over me. I reached out, grabbing Gordon's arm to steady myself. He assumed I was just reacting to all that I must be dealing with about David's death, and did not think anything of it. Part of me wanted to run back to the nurses and tell them David had been murdered and to call the police. But I did not.

As the whole picture solidified in my mind, I felt so many different emotions that I nearly screamed out loud. The feeble lady I had perceived as a friend who was harmless and nearly helpless was a cold-blooded killer. I did remember the story she told about the fire and her mother, but I had pictured a very desperate young girl who had made a horrible decision to save herself and her brother and sister.

It came to me that I had not finished telling Gordon the news about David I had learned in Florida. The phone call about David's death had interrupted me. Now, I wasn't sure if I should tell him any more about anything.

I finally spoke to the patient man who had led me to a chair. He was patting my arm with a worried look on his face. I heard him speaking and tried to come back to reality.

"Kate, it's okay, I understand. I've just gone through this, and I know how shocking and sad this news is, especially when it's delivered so unexpectedly."

As he spoke those words a new thought swept through my mind, and I hoped I was only jumping to a terrible conclusion. I knew I could not start a relationship with this man and keep the truth to myself. I asked him to take me to the floor where Mary Anne had been before her death.

"What? Are you sure about that? I don't understand."

"Gordon, I must find out something. I will explain later."

We entered the elevator and I could see he was worried. He really wanted to ask what was going on.

I tried to ease his concern. "Really, I may be thinking something that is totally untrue, but I have to find out for sure. I promise I won't keep you in the dark."

When we arrived at the proper wing of the facility we walked up to the nurse's station, and it was obvious they were happy to see Gordon.

"Dr. Livingston, it is so nice to see you. We miss your visits!"

Gordon turned and introduced me as his "friend, Kate." He briefly explained that I had just lost my husband, and the three nurses expressed their sympathy. We stood and made small talk for a few minutes.

I assumed they thought I was in deep grief and did not question the crazy look that must have been on my face.

I fumbled inside my purse for my phone and pulled up the photos I had taken when Grace and I were in Chicago. I showed some of them to the nurses and asked, "Did any of you see this lady on this floor while Mary Anne was still here?"

All of them passed the phone around and I could tell right when the tall redhead remembered.

"Mrs. Williams, that was Mary Anne's dear little aunt. Do you know her, too? She visited several times in those last weeks and seemed very sad to see her niece so out of touch. She would slip in to sit with her at the oddest hours."

I had been hoping that I was wrong with my suspicions, but there was little doubt left in my mind now. I managed a polite smile and told Gordon I was suddenly very tired and must go home. When we were finally in the elevator again, I totally broke down in deep sobs. Gordon gathered me into his strong arms and did not say a word. He must have been very confused by now.

I really was totally exhausted, but I had to say something. When we reached the first floor, I pulled Gordon into the sunny atrium and motioned for him to sit down.

"Gordon, I don't think you will understand most of this until I tell you everything that has happened since I first met Grace and Jack months ago, last autumn. I'm not totally certain, but am very suspicious about what really happened to David and Mary Anne."

I explained about Grace's recent interest in finding mushrooms, and went on to tell the old family legend about their possible use. Gordon sat and shook his head in disbelief, obviously upset. I continued, trying to figure out what to do.

"It is too late tonight, and so much has happened today. I have to go and confront her, but I need to think about what I want to say. Even if she is somehow responsible for their sudden deaths, I don't know what to do. I really can't imagine turning her in to the police at her age. If she did not confess, I doubt if anything could be proven, anyway. And I have to be honest. I am skeptical of those old stories. The mushrooms might make someone pretty sick, but I'm not sure they would cause immediate death. What do you think?"

"Speaking as a doctor, I am thinking the victim would just throw them up, and maybe feel really ill, but I can't imagine they would be lethal. Although, I have to admit I have no real knowledge of them. It all does seem really strange, though. You will have to be careful about how you approach the subject. Do you want me to go with you?"

"Oh, no," I replied, "I have to be as normal as I can. But I must know the truth. I also have to wonder if Jack knew about any of it. I need to try and sleep tonight."

"Kate, we need to go and get a bite to eat. I know you will probably not have much appetite, but I insist you try."

We ended up back at the diner where we had first visited on Christmas Eve. That night seemed like a long time ago. Our smiling waitress brought us omelets, pumpernickel toast, and steaming coffee. I found myself surprisingly hungry.

I looked at Gordon, and as our eyes met, I knew I really cared about this man. If he had not died, I was prepared to try and tell David how much I now understood about his sad existence. I really believed that we had good years, and all of it had not been horrible for either of us. I didn't think there would any sense of closure now. For so long I had resented how isolated he made me feel. I now knew he was making the best of the situation. I would never know if he ever felt badly about the negative impact he had on my life.

Between bites I explained how I had told Grace all those family tales and how badly I needed to tell them when we met in the hospital waiting room.

"Kate, I totally understand. Right after Mary Anne's accident I was devastated and angry. One night, I went out to a bar and just happened to run into an old friend. After a couple of drinks, I started talking about the past and a lot of things. My buddy realized how much I needed to vent, and sat there and let me get it out. I felt better after that night. We met a few more times, and I think we helped each other. He was keeping a few things inside, also. Everyone needs a friendly ear."

This was the place in the conversation I chose to tell Gordon about what I had found out in Florida. I went on to say that it had been shocking but knowing the truth had taken away my long-embraced anger. If I hadn't discovered the secret behind our marriage, I would have never mourned David like I now could.

"I still kind of blame him for choosing me, but I think he really believed it would all work out. He always told me I was an independent, strong-willed person and perhaps he talked himself into thinking I would be a suitable partner. He just didn't have the true love for me to give."

"Kate, you'll never know why he married you. You will go crazy thinking about it. I'm just glad there are answers to most of your questions. I know you loved David, and I am sure that he cared about you as much as he could. Being gay in those days was often a sad thing. Some men openly lived the way they wanted, but here in the Midwest, many people had to hide behind a marriage, or just be alone."

My bottled-up anger at David was replaced with pity. How horrible it must have been to spend one's life in denial. I imagined the crude jokes he must have had to laugh at, and he always had to be in character.

By now it was very late, and Gordon took me home. We rode silently for the last few miles, both of us deep in thought about so many happenings. He walked me to the door and held me tightly for a few minutes. I could feel a lot of the tension slipping away. I guiltily remembered how much I had resented the fact that David never did that for me.

CHAPTER FORTY-EIGHT

E xhaustion helped me to sleep soundly, and the dogs were obviously happy to be home, so they let me snooze a little longer into the morning. It took me a few seconds to realize all that had happened and how much more was to come. This would be the last free day I'd have for a while. Holly had gone to Eric's house to spend the night, but I knew we had to come together to organize a service for David. I was barely up with the first cup of coffee in my hand when she called.

We agreed on a plan to meet downtown for an early lunch. This would normally be very difficult, but with all the other things on my mind it mainly seemed surreal. I knew I had to just get through it in character. Finding a time to go and talk to Grace would have to be postponed. I had called her the night before and quickly told her about David's death and said we would talk later. There was no other choice right now.

I was already sitting at a table in the restaurant sipping iced tea when Holly and Eric arrived together. They both hugged me and sat down quietly. I took note of the fact that they seemed closer than they had in years. Sometimes a tragedy acts as a renewal of relationships. We discussed the arrangements, and they began a trip down memory lane, laughing about many of the experiences they had shared growing up. I found myself smiling with them.

Holly said she would just stay with Eric's family while she was in town so that I could rest. Opening my mouth to protest, I quickly thought better of it. Holly usually wanted her space and didn't handle things of this nature very well. The Celebration of Life memorial service we had planned for David would be awkward for her. When she asked if it was okay with me if she looked up an old friend while she was in town, I told her it was fine. Eric had family things to take care of, and they left.

Like on so many other occasions of my life, I found myself sitting alone. I could hear David saying, "Well, you raised them that way."

When I got back into my car I decided I had to go and talk to Grace. I must know the truth before the next day. I would have to stand and try to be the grieving widow and let dozens of people hug me. There would at least be no open casket showing. I did not think I could survive that.

I pulled into the complex where Jack and Grace lived and drove around the lake. It's funny how the rest of the world seems to be going on normally while some awful thing happens to you. The maintenance man was mowing, and three of the residents were sitting on a bench, feeding the geese.

As I neared the area where Grace and Jack lived, I immediately saw a group of emergency vehicles with lights flashing and various emergency personnel nearby. I parked a block away and hastened to their home. My heart was beating rapidly as I approached. I just could not stand one more thing. What I saw first was Jack sitting on their tiny porch with his head in his hands. A stretcher was being carried to a waiting van. It was the coroner's vehicle.

I heard one of the EMT officers saying, "Poor old lady, she must have passed during the night. Her husband didn't find her until he woke up this morning."

CHAPTER FORTY-NINE

The next few days did not seem like any reasonable form of reality to me. Somehow, I had made it back to my car. I wanted to run to the Jack and ask him a million questions, but this was not the time. Calling Gordon was the thing to do. After telling him what I had witnessed, I said I had no idea what all of this meant. He was silent for a moment.

"Oh Kate, I so much wish I could be there to support you, but your children do not even know me and I really don't think you want to offer up any big explanations right now. You know that I want to be a part of your life, but you need to just find closure. But let me know if you find out anything about what happened to Grace. We may never know the truth now."

"Gordon, I have to make myself get through all of this. For months, everything was very predictable. After I met Grace and Jack, things seemed to change quickly."

"You can do this," he said. "Just know I'll be thinking of you. Allow your children to step up and take a lot off your shoulders. My son did that for me. It made us closer."

"But I don't think I can just let all of this go, Gordon. I really need to know the truth."

"Let the dust settle then try to speak to Jack. He must know something."

I went home and laid out proper clothing for David's service. Holly called to check on me and asked me to come to Eric's home for a meal later. I did want to see my grandchildren so I agreed. My daughter-in-law gave me a big hug and apologized for not calling me more often. The kids also hugged me and promised to come and see me as much as they could. I realized they were not avoiding me on purpose. They had busy lives and I never complained.

After we enjoyed a family dinner I felt a lot more relaxed. If I was acting strangely, it was easy for them to understand. We all promised to get together much more often. Once again, the conversation turned to things long in the past. Instead of voicing the sad times, we concentrated on the best holidays, birthdays, vacations, and just funny things. I left feeling this was the best possible homage to David.

As I drove home, it almost seemed possible that better times were in the future. I showered and sat down with the dogs to look through the photo albums. I had taken them along to let my children select some of the best ones to display at the funeral home. Looking at the smiling family posing for those occasions forever frozen in time, I gave silent thanks for the years we had shared. Poor David had suffered inwardly for dedicating himself to the life that was expected of him. The things I had blamed him for were beyond his understanding. He had convinced himself that just being there, and doing his duty as he saw it, was enough.

Holly called early the next morning, saying that they would pick me up in time to stop for a quick breakfast. I dressed carefully, remembering to take along some tissues. Tears were bound to be shed on this day. Holly, Eric, and his family were on time, and I felt a strange calm as I climbed into Eric's large SUV. This was one of those times when one almost denies the present day, and it does not totally sink in until much later. I had lived through a lot of those.

In deference to the pleading of the children, we chose a popular fast food chain and settled for biscuit sandwiches. The place was busy and hearing all the background noise was a good distraction. The seriousness of the day could be postponed for a little longer.

When we finally arrived at the funeral home it was nearly time for other mourners to arrive. A large photo of David was displayed at the front, surrounded by dozens of floral arrangements and other memorial gifts. A selection of our photos played in a loop on several television sets around the room. When I picked up the booklet that told the simple facts of David's life and death dates, it all became very real.

We sat and watched the television version of our life together, and the expected tears came to all of us. Holly gripped my hand tightly, and I knew she was not really prepared to face this. Sudden death is a merciful way to go, but it leaves the survivors in denial for the first few days.

An endless line of colleagues, friends, and neighbors began to move toward us. I put on my best Kate smile through the tears and accepted the whispered comments of sympathy as well as many hugs and cheek kisses. After about an hour my hand ached from the hearty handshakes, and my legs began to hurt from standing in one spot for so long. I regretted the uncomfortable shoes I had chosen.

Holly and Eric had their own group of friends who had come to offer comfort for them. By now, Holly was weeping openly. Eric's wife and the children had gone into the area reserved for family to get drinks and escape for a little while. By mid-afternoon, the stream of people had thinned out. There were still a few small groups sitting around in quiet conversation.

A balding, middle-aged man walked up to me with a nervous look on his face. He put out his hand and said, "Mrs. Williams, I am so sorry to interrupt. I know this is a really bad time. I am Grace and Jack's son Charlie, do you remember me?"

He didn't wait for an answer, continuing as though he wanted to quickly say what he had come for.

"My dad insisted I come and talk to you. I suppose that by now you know my mother also passed away. It is just horrible, both deaths occurring within a day or so. I know you must be in total shock."

"We met on Thanksgiving last year, and I could tell even then you were close to my parents. We aren't sure what exactly happened to mom, but our doctor thinks it was a heart attack. At her age he wasn't surprised, and we did not want an autopsy."

"She had been frail for a long time, even though being around you seemed to perk her up. My dad is inconsolable right now. They were so close. We'll be having a service for her in a few days, and I hope you can come. She would have wanted you there."

My heart had begun to beat so fast that I thought I would pass out on the floor. I managed to tell this poor man how sorry I was about his mother, how much I would miss her, and I also assured him I would be at Grace's funeral. Charlie again extended his sympathy to me, and left, promising to send me the details.

After the last of the mourners left we got back into Eric's vehicle and hurried to the airport so Holly would not miss her flight back to Florida. I begged her to stay a little longer, but her husband was due home the following morning and she needed to see him. I hugged her tightly and promised I would visit her again soon. As we watched her plane take off, I was sure a little part of my heart went with her.

CHAPTER FIFTY

The following day began with an unseasonably cold rain. I had intended to go and talk to Jack, but instead I lingered in my pajamas and made pancakes. I most definitely felt the need for a little self-pampering. I decided I should call Gordon and tell him about the unforgettable day I had just spent saying goodbye to my husband. His ashes would be given to us at a later date.

He answered on the second ring and I could hear the concern in his voice.

"Kate, I wanted to come and be with you so badly yesterday, but I knew it was not a good idea."

"I'm just relieved it is behind me. However, I still have to go to the visitation for Grace in a few days."

I told Gordon about the visit from Charlie, and how I wanted to go and see Jack, but was also dreading it.

"Please let me go with you. You've had to do too much alone. I know your children and others were there, but you couldn't confide so many things and that must have been very difficult."

"Oh, Gordon, I appreciate your offering to go, but I don't think Jack would feel comfortable if you were there. I have to ask some very hard questions. I sure do hope he knows."

We chatted on for a few minutes as I started some laundry,

washed the dishes, and took care of the dogs. I had not un-packed my bags from the Florida trip yet.

By noon the rain had stopped. I put on my warm all-weath-er coat and got in the car. I tried to compose some questions in my mind, but it seemed better to just speak naturally. I realized I had mostly talked to Grace in all of the past months. Jack and I really hadn't exchanged all that many words.

When I pulled up to their place, two unfamiliar cars were parked outside. I almost did not stop, but knew that I must.

I knocked on the door and a young girl answered the door. I recalled she was a granddaughter. I explained who I was, and she seemed to remember me. Several family members were crowded into the tiny living room. It seemed so strange not to see Grace in her usual chair.

Charlie was cleaning up the kitchen as I entered. He saw me and said that Jack was in the bedroom. I offered to come back, but he was adamant as Jack was eager to speak to me. I felt so terribly sorry for the old man when I saw him. His shoulders were drooping down even more than usual, and he skin appeared almost gray. His hair wasn't combed and I had the crazy thought about how that would have upset Grace.

He made his way to one of the chairs and motioned for Charlie to come to him.

"Son, I hate to ask you, but can you take the children out for ice cream or something? I need to speak to Kate alone."

Charlie looked surprised, but he wanted to do everything he could for his father, so they all got up and got into one of the cars. I had met most of them at Thanksgiving, so there was no need for introductions.

As they drove away I went to Jack, gave him a big hug, told him how devastating the week had been, and tried to say all the proper things.

He asked for a glass of water, then took a deep breath.

"Kate, I have to tell you about Grace and explain all she has done. I will rest better for whatever life I have left if you know the full truth."

"First of all, you know how much I loved that peppery old woman. We had a lot of history. She was so happy after she met you, and had started to think of you as a daughter — or at least a little sister. She got all wrapped up in the story you told us about your family and the past. For a lot of years, there had not been much going on in our lives. After our children were adults, we put a lot of things behind us."

"I know she told you about the fire and much of what went on during this time. I was surprised she opened up about that part of her life. I don't think even our children know the things she told you. Maybe it was time for her to get it out."

"Jack, I understand. That is the reason I started telling my story the first night we met. I too needed to talk. Grace must have had a hard time in those days."

"Well, there's much more to some of the stories she told you. Even though she was only a little kid when she set that fire, she always believed that no matter what, there was a way to fix things if you were brave enough."

"I know she told you the story about how her poor sister had a better life after that horrible first husband fell in the barn and was killed. Grace knew her sister was at work with plenty of witnesses, so she hid in the hayloft and pushed that man to his death."

"After that, it became obvious to her that nobody had to just let life happen to them. There was always a way to make things better. It was years before she confessed this to me. I was totally shocked at first, but loved her so much. Most of this happened long before I knew the truth."

"Jack, I never heard the whole story of how the two of you got together. She had started to explain that she was married before, but never finished."

"Kate, when she learned I was back, and we started seeing

each other behind her husband's back, I realized it was a difficult problem. If she divorced him, she would be flat broke, and I only had a part time job. Every time we were together, I sensed her desperation."

"One day, I had to go out of town to work at a temporary job. I stopped at a little diner to get a cup of coffee on the day I returned and heard some ladies talking about how something awful had happened to their florist."

"I started listening and figured out that Grace's husband had suffered several bee stings and died before he could get help. At the time I never suspected Grace had masterminded his death. I loved her, and after a few months, we started to see each other. We have been together ever since."

"When we married I was the happiest man on earth. We ran the florist shop for a while and it was very successful. After a few years, I got a job at the new factory that was built over in Kingston. It paid well, and by then, our children were here."

"She continued to run the shop with an employee, but finally sold it. I was happy she could stay home. Her life had been so difficult earlier, and problems seemed to follow her. We had a silly argument one night, and without thinking she blurted out, "Jack, you have no idea what I did out of love for you!"

By this part of his story I had begun to feel sick. I always sensed Grace somehow managed to get her way, but I had no idea how far this went.

"She then sarcastically asked if I had any idea how hard it was to catch a dozen bees." Jack seemed to shrink into his chair as he said this.

CHAPTER FIFTY-ONE

I listened in horror as Jack related the story of how Grace had locked her unsuspecting husband into bathroom and unleashed a jar of bees inside with him. Jack shut his eyes when he spoke about how he had envisioned this. Grace had to have stood outside the door for a long time, listening to that poor man scream as he was stung over and over. When he finally fell silent, she attached a long rope to the door and hid behind a screen as she pulled it open. The bees flew out of the bathroom, most going out an open window.

When Grace figured out it was safe to come out, she took a fly swatter to kill any remaining bees then entered the bathroom. Gasping his last breaths, that poor man looked at her with pleading eyes. She did not call for help until he was gone.

"I was unprepared to hear such a story, and could not even speak to her for a long time. Grace actually seemed proud of what she had done, and told me how she had cleared the path to our life together."

I must have had a look of utter surprise on my face, because Jack reached out and patted my hand.

"Kate, I really am sorry to burden you with all of this, but you need to hear it. As years passed I stopped thinking about it, but I always remembered. Most people adored gentle little

Grace and I loved her with all of my heart. I found a way to justify her actions. We never spoke of it again. However, on the night she told me, I made her promise to never think of doing anything like that in the future."

"She seemed to need to say something else, and that's when she told me about her sister's husband. In time, I forgave her actions because I wanted to."

I had to ask the dreaded questions that I had come for.

"Jack, I have to ask. Did she have anything to do with the deaths of David and Mary Anne?"

The man placed his head into his hands and slowly began to weep. It was a few minutes before he was able to continue. I tried to wait patiently, but it was very hard to keep myself from screaming at this point.

Jack finally looked up and continued.

"As I said, Grace was very taken with you that first night. She seemed to become younger and her walking improved. I was glad of that and encouraged her to see you more. When you told the story about the mushrooms, she couldn't stop talking about it."

"But, Jack", I protested, "these were just old family legends. I never really believed it all happened that way. My grandmother Frances loved to tell stories, but I always suspected that much of it came out of her imagination. I never really knew if any of it was true."

"Well, Grace believed every word, and she was thrilled when you met Gordon. It was like the plot of a movie, she said. She was determined to figure out a way for you to be happy again with this new man."

"I had not seen her this worked up for years, but was glad she could find a way to enjoy a little drama. For many years we had been living a rather boring existence. After we moved to this place, a lot of our previous life was a closed book."

I looked back at our conversations and remembered how

her bright blue eyes had glittered when I told her what was going on. I thought back to the night Gordon had been at my house when Mary Anne died. Grace knew I would be his alibi, if he ever needed one.

As if he were reading my thoughts, Jack began to speak of that night.

"I had no idea what was going on the night Gordon's wife passed away. Grace had nagged me all day to drive her to Pine Haven. She told me an old friend had recently been taken there, and she wanted to go and see her. I wasn't all that keen on driving because I don't see very well at night anymore. But we did go, right after she gave me my insulin shot."

"I waited downstairs in the lobby during the visit. There was a good ball game on, and she wasn't gone very long. I later remembered how she had been a little wild-eyed when she came off the elevator, but I figured it was having to see a friend being confined to that place."

"I didn't find out about Mrs. Livingston's death until much later. In fact, after weeks had gone by, Grace herself muttered something about how this woman was 'out of the way,' and 'why couldn't David just pass away, too.'"

"I got curious and called the paper to find out when that woman died. After learning it was the night Grace had gone to Pine Haven, I was very suspicious. But I did not want to believe she had done this."

"Grace sometimes gave me more of my sleep meds than I am supposed to take, but I tried to watch what she did."

"Oh, Jack, you always seemed so tired!" Everything was making more sense now.

"On the night that David died, I woke up and it was already very late. My afternoon nap had lasted a long time and I felt drugged. I was a disorientated for a few minutes but then realized Grace was not there. I was thinking of calling her phone just as she came in."

"I began to ask questions, and she said she had called an Uber to take her to Pine Haven. I was shaking my head, asking why she went, and so on. There was no cover up this time. She began to ramble, as much to herself as to me."

I sat in silence as he spoke.

"Grace said something like, 'I tried that mushroom soup and it didn't work! Kate told me those mushrooms were deadly. I even stole a lot of her dried ones when she changed clothes at her house one night. I purposely spilled iced tea on her so I would have time to get them. I took that and some of the newly picked ones and made a great soup, but that stupid husband of hers wouldn't even eat much. It didn't have any effect at all! I ended up having to fix him the same way I did Dr. Livingston's wife!'"

CHAPTER FIFTY-TWO

Jack related all of this to me as best he could remember the conversation. I imagine this was pretty close to what Grace had actually said. I remembered the interest she had taken in the past to the mushroom soup stories as well as the expression on her face when she learned of my interest in Gordon. I am sure that she truly believed her intervention was going to "fix" my life.

"Jack, how did Grace die? I have to know. I swear I will never tell anyone."

The frail man looked me in the eye and said, "Kate, please understand that I truly adored Grace. I loved her from the first minute I saw her walking down that road all those years ago. But I could not let her cause any more premature deaths. Who knows, she could have decided to hasten me along some day."

"She's been giving me my insulin shots for a long time and was very good at it. I think she used it to kill Mary Anne as well as David. A quick shot between the toes wouldn't have raised any eyebrows when someone is already dying, nor with an old lady."

"I first put some of my sleeping meds into her tea. She never felt a thing."

Tears began to stream down my cheeks now. I would never have told my story had I known it would result in three deaths.

"Kate, I am going to go home with Charlie for a little while. I suspect I'll have to move into Pine Haven before long. I just want to have some time with Charlie and his family before I go. But he can never know the truth about his mother. He worshipped her, you know."

I figured out Grace had been over-dosing Jack on some type of meds for a long time. He seemed so much more alert now.

I hugged this poor old man for a long time before I left. I told him that if he ever needed anything to be sure and call me.

"Jack, believe me, your information will never leave my lips. I totally understand, and I so much appreciate your trusting me with the truth. It eases my mind so much, even though it is horrible at the same time."

"Are you sure none of it can be traced back?"

"Nobody questioned it for even a minute."

Charlie and his family were just returning as I walked to my car. I told him to please contact me if anything happened to Jack.

I needed to call Gordon with an update after my visit. But what to say? He was a doctor and could probably accept the deaths were natural. I did not want to lie to him, but had promised Jack.

I waited until I got home and entered his number into my phone. He answered right away.

"Okay, so I was just letting my imagination run away with me. Poor Grace didn't do anything wrong. Her death is just an ironic coincidence. Please forgive me for going crazy!"

"Kate, you've had so much to deal with lately. I am not surprised you thought something was wrong. I just hope all of the sadness and drama is over."

I wasn't lying when I told him I was too tired to talk any more that night.

I stared at my violet-covered tureen as I sipped my evening tea. I imagined several of my grandmothers were smiling down at me. I will never know if any of the old legends were true, but I will never repeat them again.

EPILOGUE

During the next few months, Gordon and I started to casually date and officially met each other's family. Holly and Eric seemed happy that someone had come along to make me happy. He gave me an engagement ring the following Christmas. It seemed like a very long time since we had met by chance in that elevator the previous year.

Gordon had taken me back to our favorite diner where we had shared that first cup of coffee. He reached across the table and took my hand as he presented a little ring box.

On a beautiful spring day the following year, we had a simple ceremony in the tiny hospital chapel. The Smithsons came up from Atlanta, and both our families were there as well as Marci, her mother, and other old friends. I wanted to ask Jack, but thought better of it.

During our honeymoon in Florida we walked along a moonlit beach, hand in hand, and I was happily at peace. We bought a small condo near the water and I am able to see Holly when we spend the winters there. Mollie and Daisy love running in the sand.

A few years later I heard that Jack had passed away peacefully in his sleep.

NOTES FROM THE AUTHOR

Although the main characters in this book are fictional, I was inspired to write it by several things. The actual French tureen is indeed a family heirloom, passed down through my grandma Stella's family. As a child I ate oyster soup and gravies from it numerous times.

I wanted to tell the story of many "Davids" who have lived in past decades. While Kate and David are not based on actual people, I realize how many times a young gay man had no choice but to marry a woman and pretend to have a heterosexual life with her.

Two of my best friends, Ryan and Donnie, are happily married in the 21st Century. If they had lived in some previous time, I have to wonder if they would have been trapped in a very different life, as so many were.

So I dedicate this book to all of the Davids and Kates who were caught up in lifetimes of lies and sadness. I am glad we live in the slowly changing years of tolerance, understanding, and being able to love who we choose. The Davids of the future will hopefully never have to hide in the shadows of hate and prejudice.

COMING SOON

The upcoming sequel to The
French Tureen will tell more of
Kate and Gordon's life — both
past and present. Watch for
"Violets in the Snow."